P9-DOE-210

TRI-CITY AREA VOCATIONAL SKILLS CENTER
5929 West Metaline Avenue
Kennewick, Washington 99336

# "YOU HAVE TO STOP CRYING!"

Mary Jane was howling. She wanted out of that dirty place, back in her crib. She wanted her daddy.

The room blistered with the noise. Rowena couldn't think. She couldn't light a cigarette. There was no liquor, no friends, no escape. . . .

"You have to stop doing that. You have to obey me. Do what I say. Stop making trouble all the time."

Child and mother locked eyes. The younger eyes were petrified with fear while the older face was distorted in a blind fury.

Rowena's grip on the child was like iron, and her long fingernails bit deeply into Mary Jane's flesh. . . .

# MARY JANE HARPER CRIED LAST NIGHT

"Powerful, poignant, sensitive, heart-breaking . . . it demands your attention from beginning to end."
—*New York Daily News*

⊘ SIGNET                                    (0451)

# WHEN THE GOING GETS TOUGH

☐ **THEO AND ME** by Malcolm-Jamal Warner. TV's top teen star (Theo Huxtable on *The Cosby Show*) talks straight with teens about the problems they share—drugs, sex, school, friendship, parents, race, depression—in language that they use and understand. "Strong, helpful, solid advice ... without sounding preachy."—*Publishers Weekly.*
(162161—$3.95)

☐ **THAT SUMMER** by Janet Appleton. When a protected, proper girl moves out on her own, she discovers life and love. It was the summer a girl became a woman.... "Tender, tragic, funny."—*Milwaukee Journal*
(164709—$4.95)

☐ **GOODBYE, PAPER DOLL** by Anne Snyder. Seventeen, beautiful and bright, Rosemary had everything. Then why was she starving herself to death?
(168305—$3.95)

☐ **THE TRUTH ABOUT ALEX** by Anne Snyder. What does a guy do when he's straight and finds out his best friend isn't? Brad was faced with two choices—standing by his friend and losing a West Point appointment, or giving in to the disapproving pressure from his family, girlfriend, teammates and the whole town...
(149963—$2.75)

☐ **MY NAME IS DAVY—I'M AN ALCOHOLIC** by Anne Snyder. He didn't have a friend in the world—until he discovered booze and Maxi. And suddenly the two of them were in trouble they couldn't handle, the most desperate trouble of their lives....
(161815—$2.95)

☐ **ABBY, MY LOVE** by Hadley Irwin. Abby was keeping a secret about her father she should never have kept ... "Poignant ... eloquently written ... sensitively deals with incest ... an important book."—*School Library Journal*
(145011—$2.50)

Prices slightly higher in Canada

---

Buy them at your local bookstore or use this convenient coupon for ordering.

**NEW AMERICAN LIBRARY**
**P.O. Box 999, Bergenfield, New Jersey 07621**

Please send me the books I have checked above. I am enclosing $_____
(please add $1.00 to this order to cover postage and handling). Send check or money order—no cash or C.O.D.'s. Prices and numbers are subject to change without notice.

Name_____

Address_____

City _____ State _____ Zip Code _____
Allow 4-6 weeks for delivery.
This offer, prices and numbers are subject to change without notice.

# MARY JANE HARPER CRIED LAST NIGHT

by
## Joanna Lee
and
## T. S. Cook

A SIGNET BOOK

SIGNET
Published by the Penguin Group
Penguin Books USA Inc., 375 Hudson Street,
New York, New York 10014, U.S.A.
Penguin Books Ltd, 27 Wrights Lane,
London W8 5TZ, England
Penguin Books Australia Ltd, Ringwood,
Victoria, Australia
Penguin Books Canada Ltd, 2801 John Street,
Markham, Ontario, Canada L3R 1B4
Penguin Books (N.Z.) Ltd, 182-190 Wairau Road,
Auckland 10, New Zealand

Penguin Books Ltd, Registered Offices:
Harmondsworth, Middlesex, England

First Signet Printing, May, 1978
19  18  17  16  15  14  13  12  11

Copyright © 1978 by Joanna Lee
All rights reserved

REGISTERED TRADEMARK—MARCA REGISTRADA

Printed in the United States of America

BOOKS ARE AVAILABLE AT QUANTITY DISCOUNTS WHEN USED TO PROMOTE PRODUCTS OR SERVICES
FOR INFORMATION PLEASE WRITE TO PREMIUM MARKETING DIVISION, PENGUIN BOOKS USA INC,
375 HUDSON STREET, NEW YORK, NEW YORK 10014.

# MARY JANE HARPER CRIED LAST NIGHT

# CHAPTER

## I

Some children, they say, give you no clue. No clue at all to what they will be like when they grow up, as if the child and the adult were two different individuals. But this was not the case with Mary Jane Harper. One could see her future in her face—a pretty childhood, then graceless spurts of growth, a sudden and stunning adolescence, leading to the birth of a young woman of heart-twisting beauty. It was all there, the whole blueprint, to the eye which cared to look.

Her large black three-year-old eyes floated above high cheekbones as a pert little mouth bunched up to deposit dry kisses on the nose of the small kitten she cradled in her arms.

"Mommy loves Kitty . . ." she muttered softly, hugging the struggling ball of fluff. Some of the kitten's fur found its way into her mouth, and she spat it out, wiping her lips on the sleeve of her playsuit. The kitten sought to escape the instant her hold was relaxed. But Mary Jane caught it by the hind legs.

"You be a good girl now, Kitty, or Mommy spank."

"Moorarr. . . ."

"Stop that! Stop that, you bad kitty."

But the kitten had escaped and was bounding away across a patch of muddy soil which the gardener had turned up and soaked earlier that morning. Mary Jane was about to pursue her pet when she sensed something. A half second later her mother's voice rang through the house.

"Mary Jane? Where are you?"

The little girl darted into the house and was intercepted by her mother in the hallway. She was firmly guided into her bedroom.

"Your daddy's going to be here any minute. I told you to stay in your room."

"Kitty—"

"You can play with Kitty tomorrow. Oh no, not again."

Mary Jane's underpants were damp. Her mother's face grew momentarily hard with frustration as she lifted the child swiftly from the floor and deposited her in the crib. She hastily pulled the soiled underpants from the child and tossed them into a sealed plastic pail in one corner of Mary Jane's room. Clean pants were swiftly pushed onto the small child in their place.

"I don't know why you keep doing this to me, Mary Jane. You are three years old. You *know* how to use the toilet."

"I sorry, Mommy. I be good."

"All right. Now today is very important." She slipped a lacy white dress over Mary Jane's head and then proceeded to groom the child. Soft brown tresses were smoothed and curled under the gentle strokes of a bristle brush. "Everything's going to be just perfect this time, baby girl. Daddy's really going to be surprised." Ruffled socks and patent-leather shoes added to the effect—a perfect little girl child standing in her crib, clean, brushed, smiling. "There," said Mommy, "you look just like a princess in a storybook."

She smelled smoke in the living room. "Oh, God, I left a cigarette burning. I told him I'd stopped. Stay right there, Mary Jane. Don't move."

Rowena Harper dashed into the living room and found the offending half-crushed cigarette butt smoldering in a glass coaster. She swiftly extinguished it and then dumped the contents

3

of the coaster into a nearby wastebasket. A swift wipe with a paper towel cleaned ashes from the coaster, and the towel went into the wastebasket, too, covering the butts from sight. Bill wouldn't suspect if he couldn't see evidence. Or smell it—she spritzed the room lavishly with spray deodorizer. There. "Not a thing wrong this time."

"Mommy, down!" Mary Jane bellowed from her room. She wanted out of the high crib. To make mischief, no doubt. Well, she could just stay in there a few minutes until Bill. . . .

"Mommy!" Mary Jane screamed, this time with real urgency.

Rowena rushed back into the bedroom to find Mary Jane on the floor beside her crib. The carpet was too thick to allow injury, but the child was frightened and crying.

"Did you try to get out of that crib again? I told you not to move." She picked up her wailing child and, examining her, saw there was no damage done. Just another of Mary Jane's constant bids for attention. "Mary Jane, stop crying, please. Please. Please don't make trouble now. He'll be here any second now. You know Daddy hates a hassle. Please."

She carried the child to her little chair and quickly stuffed a Tootsie Roll pop into her mouth. That always seemed to do the trick.

The crying muted and gradually stopped altogether. Rowena started the tiny chair moving.

"How about Wiggly-Bear?" Rowena suggested. Mary Jane sniffled and nodded behind her lollipop. Rowena hastily found the record and dashed it onto Mary Jane's simple record player. The story lady's voice started in on the story of the baby bear who couldn't sit still.

"There. Now be a good girl and just sit there until Mommy comes back."

Rowena turned at the door and looked around the room. Yellow gingham and white organza, playthings stacked on top of scaled-down dressers and bureaus, all in perfect order. Very, very good, Rowena thought. Like a page out of a magazine. And Mary Jane, quiet for once, in her prettiest dress, listening to the record like a little lady—that was the crowning touch.

Rowena Harper was expecting her husband any moment now, and she hastily reviewed the appearance of their home for flaws in the image. No, it was spotlessly clean, thanks to Daddy. The new maid he sent to clean every day took care of the clutter of magazines and dirty glasses which offended Bill so much. The room looked perfect. Her mother's decorator had seen to that. Bill had complained that the place didn't look as if anyone lived there—and then he complained when it got messy. It was so hard to please him. And she wanted to very much. Rowena had laid out a small snack of crackers and fruit. Twin decanters next to the silver ice chest held both wine and iced tea. Mary Jane? Quiet, but for Wiggly-Bear. Cigarettes? No trace. Yes, she was ready.

He was late. He should be here. He'd better come before this state of perfection altered. Rowena's hand slipped around the neck of the wine decanter; she hastily drew it away. This is no time for a drink, stupid. But she hoped Bill would have some wine with her when he arrived. Maybe a couple of drinks and a little talk. God, how she wanted him back. This separation was destroying her. Now he would see how competently she was keeping the house and how fit she was keeping herself. She had been running in the mornings, about a half mile. Bill had said she was lazy. He said all she did was lie around and watch TV all day. Well, she'd show him now. Rowena was a tall, very beautiful young woman. There was just the hint of a pout in her mouth, and her large green eyes were guileless. Her halter tops and sweaters from high school still fitted, filled out a bit more than when she and Bill started dating in senior year. That year had been—

Stop it! Jesus, senior year? That was ancient history, girl. Think about the present: the couch, the carpet, cigarettes, Mary Jane, the doorbell.

"Hi."

"Hi."

Bill Harper was a trim, athletic young man in a tight-fitting sport shirt and tennis shorts. Over his shoulder Rowena caught a glimpse of the laundry van. Bill and his father owned a chain of prosperous dry-cleaning stores in prime locations. Still, Bill preferred the athletic look to the starched and laundered.

It was strange, welcoming your own husband to the house like a stranger. Bill's voice betrayed the awkwardness of the situation, too. "How're you doing?"

Rowena ushered him into the *Better Homes and Gardens* centerfold. She pulled her blouse down slightly to accentuate her slimness. "Great. I've been running two miles a day."

"You sure look good."

"Thanks, honey. You do, too."

"House looks real good."

"I'm doing a needlepoint pillow for the couch."

There was an awkward pause. "Really," Bill said without expression.

"Yes. . . . Have you been seeing anybody?" Rowena immediately regretted saying it. She had meant "any of the old high school gang." But Bill might take it to mean something else.

He did. "No."

"Well, me neither. I meant—"

But Bill was shooting her a long, hard glance. Please, Rowena thought, let's get off *this* subject. "Honest to God, Bill, I haven't. I miss you."

"Rowena, my mom is waiting for us," Bill said quickly. "She's got people coming."

"Bill. . . ."

"Can I get Mary Jane now?"

"Honey, I thought we could talk." Rowena said, moving toward the couch. But when she turned to invite Bill to sit down, she saw a shocked expression on his face. She followed his eyes. There in the hallway was Mary Jane, covered from head to foot with thick black garden mud.

"Hi, Daddy, Kitty went bye-bye."

Rowena screamed, "Mary Jane! What did you do to yourself?"

"I fall down. I sorry."

Mary Jane began to cry softly. Rowena looked at Bill, and she saw his face twist up into that expression she hated, that expression of accusation and disgust which he seemed to have worn more or less continually during the last six months of their marriage. Rowena turned to Mary Jane, fighting for control.

"Sure you're sorry," she screamed at her child. "You're *always* sorry. Look at you!"

There was no mistaking the tremor of anger in Bill's voice. "I told you what time I'd be here. I told you to have her ready."

"I *did* have her ready. She was all perfect." Rowena bent over Mary Jane and started tugging the muddy dress off, splattering mud on the carpet and on her own sweater. "I'll get her changed right away. It's not my fault. She just won't stay out of the dirt."

Bill was shouting. "If you would look after her like a mother is supposed to, this wouldn't keep happening."

"That's not fair. You're always blaming me. Everything's always my fault."

"We've done this number before, Rowena. I don't want it anymore." Bill slammed the door behind him, and his van roared out the driveway.

Rowena stared at the front door for a few seconds after Bill left. When she looked down at her muddy child, her face was drained, blank, expressionless as a statue's.

"You ruined it," she announced under her breath to Mary Jane, and then pushed the child ahead of her into the yellow and white nursery. The nursery door whooshed slowly closed against the thick pile of the carpet, and the lock clicked.

Dr. Angela Buccieri had actually finished her shift and was almost out the main entrance when Nurse Ramos paged her to the examination room. She bustled down the ground-floor corridor of Santa Carla General Hospital, moving briskly through knots of chatting nurses and orderlies. Dr. Buccieri was a pediatrics resident. That alone, in the Byzantine pecking order of modern hospitals, accorded her some respect, but it was her fiery temper and impatience with small talk which parted the ways for her. Angela was dark and attractive with a massive corolla of curly hair. When she strayed from her beloved pediatrics department onto other floors, she was sometimes confused for a nurse or a laboratory technician. But woe to the doctor or surgeon who did so and issued her an order. Angela was full-blooded Italian, born and reared in Brooklyn, New York, and she dearly loved to puncture the Anglo, male, UCLA-educated stereotype of the Santa Carla General staff.

This tendency to burst balloons had earned her the reputation of being somewhat abrasive and difficult. But never on her own floor. In pediatrics, Dr. Buccieri was known as an extremely skilled physician with a splendid approach to the patient. Everyone there liked her, and she, in her Italian manner, loved all of

10

them: the staff, the nurses, and, above all, the kids.

Nurse Ramos was standing over the sedated form of a child when Angela marched into the examination room. "Okay, gang," said the doctor in a voice that seemed somehow an octave too low for her frame, "what have we got?" Without waiting for an answer, Angela bent over the drowsy child. A temporary cast was bound to her right arm.

"Mother brought her in," Nurse Ramos stated. "Says she fell and broke her arm."

"That much is clear. Help me turn her. Careful. . . ."

They slowly turned the delicate brown-haired little girl over on her back. The child's large black eyes were expressionless as Dr. Buccieri began her examination. It was standard practice (*her* standard practice anyway) to examine the whole child in the case of such a serious injury. Fractures of children's bones are generally more serious and complicated than fractures of the same bones in an adult.

Dr. Bucciero palpitated the little girl's sides for uniformity and her spine for any unusual curvature. Her legs seemed well developed and the same length. As she reached around, the liver and spleen felt good. Dr. Buccieri slipped the child's underpants down for a look at the genitalia.

"Oh, no!"

The child's right buttock sported three conical burn marks. They were old and healed over but, even so, looked painful.

"Take a look at this."

"I see the marks, Doctor, but I'm not sure I know—"

"Healed-over cigarette burns is what they are, Miss Ramos. You say the mother brought her in?"

"She's waiting outside." Nurse Ramos handed her the paperwork as she departed under a full head of steam.

When she arrived at the waiting room, however, Angela took a deep breath. She was too much a professional to jump to conclusions. Her trained eye picked out the mother—young, clean-cut, nervous.

"Mrs. Harper?"

Rowena snapped her head up abruptly from a damp Kleenex. "Yes?"

"I'm Dr. Buccieri."

"My baby? Oh, God, if anything bad happens to her, I'll never forgive myself."

"Your child has a fractured arm, but it should heal without complications."

"It's all my fault."

Angela heard sincere regret in Rowena's voice. She asked softly, "How did it happen?"

"She fell out of her crib. See, she keeps trying to climb out."

"She's pretty big for a crib, isn't she?" asked the doctor, her eyes trained on Rowena's face.

"Well, she's not toilet-trained yet. I just left her for a second to open the front door."

"I see. . . . So you didn't see her fall?"

"No. I just left for a minute. It was wrong, I know."

Rowena was looking up into Dr. Buccieri's eyes so remorsefully that Angela felt herself question that which she had been sure of only a few minutes before. "Don't be hard on yourself, Mrs. Harper. These things happen." Angela waited a second before asking, "Do you smoke?"

"No. Not anymore. My husband hates cigarettes. Alcohol, too. He believes in clean living, you know? We're separated now."

"So he wasn't at home when the accident happened."

"No. Why do you ask about cigarettes?"

"Well, there are several small burns on Mary Jane's buttocks. I wondered if she might have backed into a lit cigarette?"

"Yes. A couple of times before I stopped smoking. Mary Jane is always falling, tripping, bumping into things. She's a nervous child. She cries a lot, I don't know. . . ."

Angela flipped open the folder containing the

13

admission form and made a few notes. "Mrs. Harper, from what you tell me, I think a thorough neurological workup is in order. I'd like to keep Mary Jane here at the hospital for a few days, do some more tests."

"More tests? What tests have you done?"

Angela looked up from the form. Rowena's question had a slight tone of hostility. "Just the X ray of her arm. The tests I'm thinking of include—"

"Oh, of course, I'm sorry. Whatever you say, Doctor."

"Well, I'll arrange for a room."

And then, apparently, Rowena suddenly remembered something. "Oh, wait a minute. Tomorrow is Nana's birthday. She'd be brokenhearted if Mary Jane wasn't there. If it's just tests you have to do, I'll bring Mary Jane back in tomorrow night."

"It would be my advice to leave her now," Angela suggested as firmly as she could, her mind again alert to the quick switch.

Rowena smiled sweetly. "Thank you, Doctor, but I really think she'd better come home with me."

Angela returned her smile, but not without some effort. "All right. Why don't you go down to the cafeteria and have a cup of coffee? It'll be another hour anyway."

Rowena took her advice, and Dr. Buccieri

walked back to the examining room. But she walked slowly, lost in thought. Did all the pieces fit, or was she reaching? Back in Brooklyn the incidence of child abuse, neglect, or battery had been quite high, and the evidence usually overwhelming. It hadn't been difficult to diagnose child abuse when the parent arrived at the hospital drunk and attempted to kick the pediatrician. That had actually happened, and Angela had suffered a sprained foot to prove it. Rowena Harper was not that kind. Still, some of the signs were there.

Angela Buccieri, daughter of a longshoreman and the eldest of five children, had become a doctor only through long hard study and incredible desire. Along the way, between jobs and night classes, she had attended many lectures on child abuse, and they had proved to be some of the most valuable hours she had spent behind a notebook. Item: On first interview the abusing parent usually arrives alone, without support from the other. Item: Most abusing parents live in physical or emotional isolation from their spouses or the community. Rowena Harper fitted most of this description. Item: Young mothers are prime candidates, particularly those who wanted a "baby" but not necessarily a "child." Rowena was young and seemed to consider Mary Jane her "baby," even though the child was three years old.

Item: Parent often complains that the child is nervous and clumsy. Item: Parent often claims the child is backward in some way, such as toilet training. Item: Parent is often very open about marital troubles or stress but tends to close up when stress centered on the child is mentioned. Dr. Buccieri had received a thumbnail sketch of Mary Jane's father, but Rowena had shied away from discussing the cigarette accidents. Item: Parent rarely allows child to remain in hospital care, even for tests.

When Angela arrived back at the examining room, these items fell into place. The X ray of Mary Jane's fracture was developed. It revealed a spiral fracture of the right humerus. Most home accidents produce lateral clean breaks, like snapping a carrot in half. This one twisted in a long spiral nearly a quarter of the bone's length.

"Hi there. My name's Angie. What's yours?"

"Mary Jane." The sedative was beginning to wear off now. Angie's smiling face leaned over the bed. "Where's Mommy?"

"Right outside, honey. What happened to you?"

Mary Jane looked at the doctor for a moment, but then tears began to form in her eyes. Angela reached over and stroked the child's hair gently. "Won't you tell me how you got yourself hurt?"

16

And then it appeared. It was what Dr. Buccieri called the Mask. Mary Jane stopped crying. Her face went blank, and she turned her head toward the wall. She said nothing. Her silence was the most positive clue of all. Protecting her mother. Most abused children do. Angie nodded to herself. "Okay, Mary Jane. You rest now."

Dr. Orrin Helgerson was director of the department of pediatrics at Santa Carla General Hospital, and his office was a splendid showroom of teak furniture and objects in brass and porcelain. Both sides of his family for three generations had been Swedish, and Dr. Helgerson's appearance was a textbook study of the Swedish physique—tall, sturdy, with a strong frame and a ruddy complexion. He had a positive and rational mind, able to penetrate problems with a natural force of will. But he did not treat all facets of life with this scientific objectivity. While not a stuffy man in general, Dr. Helgerson did require some measure of propriety in his life. He insisted on the proper titles and adhered closely to those unspoken standards and deferences known as medical courtesy. Thus, he was greatly annoyed when a short dark-complexioned female doctor burst into his office without so much as a swipe at the door. Nor was Dr. Helgerson the kind to conceal annoyance.

Dr. Buccieri was in a hurry. "Dr. Helgerson, I suspect we have a battered three-year-old female downstairs. Mother won't let her stay. I want to order a full skeletal X ray before we release her."

"Don't you knock before you enter an office, Doctor—"

"Buccieri. Sometimes I forget. The child has a spiral fracture of the right humerus. Mother claims she fell out of a crib, but . . . we both know spiral fractures occur from pulling and twisting. Not from falling."

"Unless, of course, the child caught her arm in the blankets or in the rung of the crib and it got twisted as she fell," Dr. Helgerson suggested in a professional tone of voice.

Dr. Buccieri answered like a rebellious student from the back row. "That would be very unusual, wouldn't it?"

Dr. Helgerson picked up his phone and buzzed for the secretary. Angela looked around his office for a moment, trying to conceal her impatience.

"Lillian? Call my wife, tell her I'm running ten minutes behind."

"Better tell her an hour," Angela interrupted. The department head glared at her. "Excuse me, but there's more. The child has cigarette burns on her buttocks. The mother claims she got them accidentally."

There was a short pause, ice-covered. "Where did you take your training, Doctor—?"

"Bu-Chair-Ee. St. Anthony's Hospital in Brooklyn, why?"

"That's a ghetto area, is it not? With a high preponderance of trauma owing to crimes of violence?"

"Yes. So?"

"Look around you, Dr. Bu-see-erie." Dr. Helgerson was still having trouble with the name. Or was he being purposefully snide? "This is not Brooklyn."

Angela fought to keep cool and lost. "I don't care if it's Geneva, Switzerland. I have a little girl downstairs with a broken arm, and there's a good chance that the mother did it. All I want from you is permission to X-ray the child's whole body to see if there are any healed-over fractures before I release her. Okay?"

Helgerson's face was tight, but he said, "I'll take a look."

He followed Angela's compact form through his outer office and onto the pediatrics floor. But about halfway to the examining room where Mary Jane was waiting, Angela heard Helgerson stop in his tracks and cry out, "Rowena? Is that you?"

Rowena Harper was sitting on a wooden bench near the elevator. Angela saw relief wash over the young woman's face as she swiftly rose and rushed into the arms of Dr. Helgerson.

"Oh, Dr. Helgerson," Rowena sobbed. "I'm so glad you're here. Mary Jane got hurt . . . I just left her for a minute . . . she fell out of her crib."

Helgerson patted Rowena on the head and comforted her, but his eyes were shooting fire at Angela over the young woman's shoulder. "There, there . . . I know that little wiggleworm. Got herself all twisted up and took a header, huh?" He issued orders to Angela in a voice that almost hissed. "Get our best orthopedics man down here right away. I want our little girl attended to and out of here in an hour."

He whispered a few more words of comfort to Rowena and then strode past a disbelieving Dr. Buccieri toward the examining room. Angela and Rowena stared at each other, and Angela was certain she saw an infuriating smugness in Rowena's eyes.

When she arrived at the examining room, Dr. Helgerson had just finished studying Mary Jane's X rays and was paternally stroking Mary Jane's smooth brown hair. Angela shot a glance at Nurse Ramos and then approached the patient. "You're not going to do the full skeletal?"

"I am not," said Helgerson, studying the child.

"I'll bet you a hundred dollars that mother is lying."

Helgerson whirled around. That was the trouble with doctors who trained in the inner city. They learned to believe the worst about people. They never learned to relax even where the streets were free of crime. "Now you listen here. I have known Rowena Atherton all of her life. She went through school with my daughter. Her father is Thomas J. Atherton, one of my best friends. For you to accuse that young woman of being a child abuser is not only ridiculous, but an . . . insult to one of the finest families in this community."

Angela held her ground, despite the warning look in Nurse Ramos' eyes. "I hope they'll accept my apology," she said evenly, "but I gotta report this."

"No, Doctor, you do not." Helgerson moved closer to Angela until he was towering over her, using his physical size as a kind of intimidation. "As director of this department I expressly forbid you to pursue this matter any further, either verbally or in the medical records." He paused a few seconds to let it sink in, then brushed by Angela with an insulting *capisc'*?

Angela hadn't really been intimidated, but she hated cheap masculine tricks like that. So

she was half his size? So what? He was wrong,
and she was right. To punctuate her feelings,
she dragged her thumbnail across her front
teeth—that universally crude Italian street gesture popular even in Shakespeare's day. Her father would have beaten her silly if he'd seen
her do it, but she was a big girl now, and she
said what she felt.

And she did what she felt like doing. Or
rather, what human decency required of her.
She lifted the telephone receiver off the wall.
"Information? I want the number of Children's
Protective Services."

Nurse Ramos was at her side. "Dr. Buccieri,
he told you to drop it."

"Yeah, well, I got this problem, see? Sometimes I don't hear so good."

Ramos smiled a warm and supportive smile.
"Maybe you ought to see a doctor about that."

# CHAPTER

## II

It was a low, gray, cloudy Southern California morning. The air was cool and pleasant, filled with rare moisture—in all respects a perfect morning for jogging. When one lived for five years in a neighborhood, the morning jog became a kind of social event. Not that everyone knew everyone else. In fact, there were no words spoken. The morning jog was the realm of the "nodding acquaintance." Neighbors passed one another with a wave of the hand, a blink of the eye in greeting. Those in better shape managed a grunt.

Almost everyone knew Dave Williams. He was a black man. Actually there were several black families on his block, and Santa Carla was a well-integrated community. But Dave was the only one who jogged mornings and consequently was the best known. He was reaching the midpoint of his course and pushing hard when Mrs. Meyer, a sturdy woman in her late forties, went bobbing past going the other way. They nodded and smiled at each other.

"Hup, hup," Dave managed.

Dave rounded the top of the slight incline that marked the halfway point, crossed over to the center of the boulevard, and hit his stride, as he ran downhill on the lush grass of the center divider. Here was where he really pushed himself. Funny, he thought through the blur of sweat and exertion. Ten years ago the sight of a tall, muscular black man running through the streets of Santa Carla at 7:30 A.M. would have brought out the National Guard. Thank God for the progress of man.

Half a mile down the boulevard divider, Dave turned across the street and sprinted up the short driveway to his house. Inside, he could hear his wife making breakfast and the tumult of the boys in the bathroom. He leaned against his car for a minute to catch his breath. Marvelous feeling, he thought, to be in this kind of shape. Also marvelous, this one moment, the only moment of the day in which he would not be aware that he wanted a cigarette.

If only he could jog all day long, quitting would be easy.

Behind the garage was a small glassed-in room where Dave pursued his oil painting. A large canvas was resting against the wall. Dave touched the back of his index finger across the bottom of the abstract cityscape, the part he remembered painting last. It was dry. Since most all available wall space in their house was taken, this one was going to the office. He carried it around and carefully deposited it in the back of his red station wagon. He then chased the boys from the bathroom, showered, shaved, checked his never-varying weight on the scales, and deposited a kiss on Jeannie's lips.

"No breakfast?"

"I'm late. See you tonight."

Dave Williams, thirty-five years old, was a social worker at the county Department of Children's Protective Services. A long, low brick building on Seventh Street, doled directly from the federal pork barrel, was headquarters for county services in the Santa Carla area. Social welfare had been Dave's major at the university, and he was very good at his job. He was big and imposing physically, a fact which usually assured him an attentive audience, but his face exuded concern and kindness, which won him friends. He had been told he was very articulate on certain subjects, particularly child abuse. That pleased him. Dave Williams was a man who loved children.

When he entered his government-issue office, there was a young woman in a white coat waiting for him.

"Hi. I'm Dave Williams."

"Dr. Angela Buccieri, Santa Carla General."

"Morning. Wait a minute, here. . . ." Dave located the picture hook he'd pounded into the wall the day before and carefully hung his painting on it. The drab room visibly brightened.

Dr. Buccieri stood behind him as he straightened it. "I really like that painting, Mr. Williams. Did you do it?"

"Yeah. I'm the last of the great Sunday painters."

"It's like the lights of a city, right?"

Dave was unable to hide his pleasure. The painting was, after all, somewhat abstract. "That's right." He slid in behind his desk and reached behind him to a glass jar full of licorice sticks. One went into his mouth; another was offered to Angela. "For that"—Dave smiled—"you deserve a prize."

"Trying to stop smoking, huh?"

Dave chuckled. "Sounds like you've been there. Well, Doctor, what can I do for you?"

Angela told him in straight, uncomplicated language about Mary Jane Harper and her suspicions. Dave Williams nodded and made notes as she spoke. It was clear to Angela that she'd come to the right person and obvious from the way he nodded and the questions he asked that he agreed with her suspicions. Finally, Dave said, "Okay, Doctor. I'll start the investigation you request tomorrow. But one thing I'm curious about."

"What's that?"

"How come you're here in person? Why didn't you just make your report over the phone?"

Angela studied Dave Williams for a moment. He seemed like a very concerned individual, one who was not above breaking a rule here or there if it meant saving a child some pain. She couldn't be sure, of course—the social welfare bureaucrats in New York City had been in love with titles and salaries and little else. But she felt on common ground with this large black man with the sweet face. "I'll tell you," she said finally. "It's because this report is unauthorized. The director of pediatrics has known the mother since childhood. A friend of the family. He says I'm crazy and should drop it."

Dave put down his pencil. A grin was building behind his observant eyes. "Dr. Buccieri," Dave asked slowly, "how many female residents are there at General?"

"Two."

27

"And you're aiming to make it one?"

"I'm a street kid, Mr. Williams. I can smell when things aren't right. And between that mother and that child things are not right. I can't drop it."

Dave rose from his chair. "I hear you, Doctor." He extended his hand. "My first name is Dave."

Angela rose to shake his hand. "Angie. Man, are you tall!"

Dave Williams arrived at the Harper home at about two-thirty that afternoon. It was in a section of Santa Carla very much like his own, with large ranch-style houses and scattered oak trees among the palms. As was his habit, he parked his car a few doors away and walked to the address. It gave him a chance to get the feeling of the neighborhood.

Dave knew a lot about neighborhoods. He'd lived in a wide variety in his time. They got under his skin. He'd grown up, for example, in a pleasant part of Pasadena. His father ran a funeral home in that city and did a good business. Their neighborhood was well maintained and comfortable with very little racial prejudice. Dave had been readily accepted in the school system along with several other black children. He had never worried about much during his childhood in Pasadena, and his high

28

school days had passed in a happy blur of social, academic, and athletic triumphs.

And then he woke up one morning and saw smoke. Mountains separated Pasadena from the city, so he jumped into his 1962 green Chevy convertible and drove up into the hills for a better look.

What was burning was Watts.

Dave Williams kept driving. He drove through the streets of Watts during the riots. He found incredible anger, numbing poverty, paralyzing ignorance. He found no hope, no action, no concern from the state. He had known it was there before, of course, but somehow it got to him, just like the thick white smoke from the fires. Dave Williams found work in Watts. He found a social conscience.

He lived in Watts for the next three years, working as an assistant to the Watts Community Council. That was where he had met Jeannie and where they had married. Later, when he went to school for his degrees, she supported them on her salary as a factory worker.

And now here he was walking a beat in Santa Carla, a nice middle-class community. Was it a cop-out? No, he didn't honestly think so. He knew, and Jeannie knew also, that someday they'd be returning to the inner city. Right now he wanted a few years under his belt with the county. He wanted some seniority and some clout. Then maybe, with some weight to throw around, he could really shake things up.

Also, there was work to be done here. When they'd first moved to Santa Carla, the quiet streets and innumerable playgrounds seemed unreal to them. But he'd come to realize that things are the same anywhere the vital human emotions were involved. It seemed unbelievable that families in Santa Carla could have the same kind of lacerating emotional and psychological problems that the citizens of Watts did.

But the Santa Carlans did. And he had a bulging file cabinet of case histories to prove it.

The man living next door to the Harpers was watering his lawn as Dave passed. "Afternoon," Dave offered.

The man nodded and looked away. Dave felt like informing him that he was in violation of the Los Angeles water conservation program by watering in the afternoon, but he passed on. If there was evidence of child abuse at the Harpers', these neighbors might be called on as witnesses. It was hard enough to get testimony without antagonizing them.

Westminster chimes sounded in the Harpers' house as Dave pushed the doorbell. He straightened his coat and tie. Experience had taught him one firm lesson: Never anticipate. There was no telling how Mrs. Rowena Harper would look, speak, act. Like the population at large, the people Dave contacted in cases like this were of infinite variety. If one harbored expectations or stereotypes, one would flounder.

The door swung open. "Mrs. Harper?"

"Yes."

Sure enough, no rules. Rowena Harper looked like the perfect mother. She was young, very attractive, and presided over a home which looked clean and well organized. Nor was there a trace of defensiveness or racism in her voice. She smiled pleasantly and brushed hair away from her eyes.

"My name is Dave Williams. I work for the Children's Protective Services. I wonder if I might talk to you?"

"Sure. Come in."

Dave closed the front door behind him and stood in the small foyer. Despite her initially friendly greeting, Rowena was not inviting him all the way in. She became a little more businesslike now. "What's Children's Protective Services?"

"Well, it's a sort of catchall title for a bunch of different services. For example, we do a routine follow-up when kids have accidents."

"What do you mean a follow-up?"

She was wary now, but Dave was a master at defusing situations. "We have a variety of free services. Your taxes pay for it, so we like to let you know what's available. For example, there's— Oh, boy!" Dave flared his nostrils in the direction of Rowena's kitchen. "Do I smell chocolate chip cookies?"

Rowena smiled. "Yeah. I just put them in the oven."

Dave moved toward the smell and then into the living room, anything to get out of the foyer and into the house. The room was really very elegant and clean. He could imagine Mrs. Harper entertaining dozens of equally athletic and attractive young people, laughing, enjoying themselves. "I'm trying to stop smoking, you see, and it's killing me. Can't stop eating. Really a nice place you have here. Could I see Mary Jane's room?"

"She's sleeping."

"I'll just take a quick look." Rowena stared at Dave for a moment and then led him in the direction of the little girl's room. "You see, that's one of my hats: home safety. You'd be surprised at the accidents that happen because of cleaning stuff left around, or even dangerous toys."

"I'm very careful about that," Rowena offered.

Mary Jane Harper was asleep in her crib, her tiny right arm swathed in a plastic cast and sling. Dave poked his head through the door and scanned the shelves and floor. His heart beat just a bit faster as he quickly took in the thick, luxurious, heavily padded wall-to-wall carpeting. Click. There it was. He kept his smile on.

"Pretty room," Dave offered when they were back in the living room again. "Jeannie . . . that's my wife . . . she'd just flip over that yellow carpet." He felt the nicotine urge and popped a licorice drop into his mouth. Rowena declined when offered one. "We have three kids. All boys. Our place looks like a downtown gym. Must be a lot easier just having one."

She reacted, just a bit of her assurance falling away.

"Not necessarily . . . I mean, some babies cry so much they might as well be three." Rowena tossed back her head as if she were looking to God for confirmation.

"Mary Jane cries a lot, does she?"

"All the time! Especially the last six months since her daddy left us."

"Oh, I didn't realize you were all alone." Actually Dr. Buccieri had related this fact to him, along with Rowena's description of her baby who cried all the time. Dave wanted to hear it from the source.

"Well, we are. All alone. And Mary Jane seems to miss him a lot. I mean, he never lifted a finger to do anything for her while he was living here, but once he was gone you'd think the world ended or something."

It was a strange little speech, Dave thought, equal parts frustration, courage, and contempt. He thought he heard a cry for help somewhere in there. At the risk of losing her, he decided to offer the help she might need. He pulled a white business card from his breast pocket. "May I call you Rowena?"

"Sure."

"Okay. Look, one of my other hats . . . I want to let you know there are places you can go if you feel the pressure building."

"What do you mean?"

"Hey, it's not easy raising a child with two parents. But alone, especially if you're young, it can really be tough. Here."

He held out the card to Rowena, and she took it. "Sometimes," Dave continued, "just talking it out with other people like yourself can help a lot." Dave started slowly for the door.

"Oh, thank you. Thank you very much," Rowena said, escorting Dave to the foyer. "I think those cookies are about ready. They're just the frozen kind, but they're good. It's no trouble."

Dave smiled broadly as he stepped onto the front porch. "Next time."

"Okay," Rowena said, smiling back at him. She closed the door. The smile faded from her face. "Trouble," she said to herself.

Since Bill's ill-fated visit, the decanter on the bar had been refilled with its customary contents—bourbon. She poured herself a tall glass and drank it down slowly, nervously, looking over the rim of the glass at the card Dave had left. "PARENTS ANONYMOUS" said the largest line of type. Parents Anonymous?

The bourbon burned in her throat, and she slammed the glass back down on the bar. Rowena lit a cigarette, took a puff, stubbed it out.

"*I'm* in trouble."

The house was as silent as a grave. Three o'clock in the afternoon and not a sound. Just me drinking booze. At three o'clock in the after—

Mary Jane woke up in the yellow nursery and began to cry. The sound penetrated Rowena like an unseen force, causing her to tremble like a crystal goblet left too close to the stereo speaker.

"She's *always* getting me in trouble!" The child's cries grew louder and more insistent. "Someone make her shut up!"

And then Rowena was in the nursery at Mary Jane's cribside, her screams competing with her baby's.

"Shut up!"

The crying stopped. Mary Jane Harper lay still, curled up in a fetal position with her small

35

face to the wall. Rowena dragged her around to face the room.

"Look at me when I'm talking to you. Why do you keep doing this to me?"

Child and mother locked eyes. The younger eyes were petrified with fear while the older face was distorted in a blind fury.

"Why?"

Rowena's grip on the child was like iron. Her long fingernails bit deeply into Mary Jane's flesh.

"Why?"

When Dave returned to his office, the first thing on his agenda was a call to Santa Carla General Hospital and Angela Buccieri. She was on the line in a matter of seconds. How easy it was to find doctors when they wanted to talk to you. Except that Angela wasn't pleased by what he had to report.

"Okay," Dave stated firmly. "The police department has no record of any previous abuse, nor does the county. The baby was sleeping like an angel in a spotless nursery, and young Mrs. Harper was open, friendly, and baking chocolate chip cookies."

There was a big disgusted sigh from the other end of the phone. "You tell me she was wearing a ruffled apron and I will throw up," Angela threatened.

"She was. Don't."

"Okay, so Helgerson was right, and I'm crazy."

"I would say so," Dave responded. He paused, thinking. "Except for one thing."

"What's that?"

"The crib that the baby allegedly fell from to get her broken arm rests on a carpet at least two inches thick."

# CHAPTER

# III

Santa Carla really was a small town, despite its sizable population. When Dave Williams arrived the next day at the address Rowena had listed for her husband on the hospital form, he found a Harper's dry cleaning store. There were several of these around town, including the one he and Jeannie used. And according to that immutable law of urban America, this one was rack-for-rack identical to the one across town.

Identical but for the large balding man who stepped behind the counter when Dave approached. "Yes, sir?"

"Yes. I'm looking for Bill Harper. I believe he works here."

The man's "customer service" smile disappeared. He looked the black man up and down. "Here and all over town. I'm Bill's dad. What do you want to see him about?"

"About his daughter." Dave handed Mr. Harper his card. "My name's Williams. I'm a social worker from the Children's Protective Services."

The man's face turned nasty. Dave expected it. When marriages break up, the pain and bitterness cascade down both family trees. "Bill don't have custody of the kid. *She* does."

"I know that, Mr. Harper. But you see, Mrs. Harper may be having some problems with Mary Jane, and I just figured the child's father should be involved."

"Well, you figured wrong. That snoot-faced kid my boy married near ruined him. I raised a clean-living boy, I can tell you. Football scholarships waiting for him at every college in the state. Hell, in the country. . . . But no, that little girl had to get herself knocked up, so my boy had to marry her." The old man's disappointment and anger had been smoldering for a long time. "And the end to all his chances."

"Mr. Harper. . . ."

"And then, after they lost the first baby, all that stuff with her drinking and running around. She made her choice. As far as I'm concerned, whatever problems that little tramp has she can take to her snoot-faced people. My boy's just starting to get himself back together now. I want her to leave him alone."

"Mr. Harper," Dave said softly, "the person I am most concerned about is three years old. She is Bill's daughter. Mary Jane. Your grandchild."

But the door chimes rang as an entering customer broke the electric eye. "Bill's on his lunch hour," Mr. Harper said quickly. "You look for him on the high school track."

And that was the end of the interview.

Santa Carla East High was just two blocks away, and Dave decided to walk. Part of his job, of course, was to fill in the background of child abuse cases, to get a feeling for the tensions which bring on such abuse. It was like a child's coloring book—people offered a very sketchy public face to strangers; he filled in the flesh tones. But this wasn't going to require much coloring. It had just been handed to him, like a sixty-second Polaroid color print. Santa Carla might be a small town, but there was still a social hierarchy. There were some very firm status lines. Rowena's family, the Athertons, were old-time Santa Carla residents, descended from pioneers. Atherton was president and chairman of the board of Santa Carla First Bank, the one downtown in the second oldest building in town. Only the Mission was more venerable. He served on the boards of half a dozen community institutions and businesses, and his wife was the *grande dame* of the social page. Old money, comfortable money, with social connections and obligations as long as your arm. Grand things had certainly been planned for Rowena—school back East, European vacations, a suitable marriage.

Dave reached the dirt track behind East High and spotted a man in his twenties running effortlessly. And then there was Bill Harper—handsome, athletic, a football hero. A couple of nights on the beach at Simpson Cove, the local parking spot, and the Athertons were meeting the Harpers one tense night over dinner. The banker and the dry cleaner, each feeling that his offspring had been seduced out of a grand future by the loose morality of the other's.

And Bill and Rowena? They soon found their house a much more confining space than the dark beach at Simpson Cove.

It was an old story, one which had been hyped to death by pulp fiction. The pulps never dwelt on the anguish of the parents, however. Or the confusion of young marrieds.

Or the broken bones of the third generation.

"Mr. Harper? Bill?"

Dave had timed his greeting to catch Harper

as he trotted by a chain-link gate. Bill stopped and saw a smiling black man in a well-tailored blazer and tie. He was immediately suspicious. "Yeah?"

"Dave Williams. Children's Protective Services. I'd like to talk to you for a few minutes, if we could."

Bill had already caught his breath. He wandered a little closer to the gate—no reason to shout this all over the playing fields. "What about?"

"Mary Jane. I assume you know she had an accident. Broke her arm."

"Yeah, I know that."

"Were you at the house that day?"

"You work for the police?"

Dave produced his card and held it up to the fence. "No, man—the county."

Bill started to walk back to the track. "I don't have to talk to you."

Dave called after him. "No, you sure don't. But . . . uh, hey, I'm not a guy who gets people into trouble. I'm a guy who just tries to find answers. Okay?"

Bill returned. "Answers for what?"

"For questions like . . . how did the accident happen?"

"You ask Rowena. That happened after I left."

Dave found his temper inching upward. This

Harper character just didn't seem to care. "Okay—uh, look, I know some kids are accident-prone. Always bumping into things, tripping, falling. Would you say that describes Mary Jane?"

"I don't know. I don't see her that often."

Dave's cool was precious to him, but he could feel it leaking away now. "Mr. Harper," he said sharply, "you may not live in the house, but you still see your child. Whatever problem we have here does not belong exclusively to Rowena. Together or apart, you are still Mary Jane's father."

Bill Harper frosted visibly. "Yeah," he said. "Maybe." He returned to the track and sprinted out of earshot.

A pair of intense brown eyes scanned the cards held inches beneath them. Then they blinked upward to find the brown eyes on the other side of the small table. The two players locked gazes for long seconds. The psychology and the bluffing were at an end. Now it was showdown—put up or shut up.

"Okay. Tell you what I'm gonna do. I'll trade you Roger Maris for Ron Cey."

"No way, Doc. You want Ron Cey, you gotta give me Maris *and* Mantle."

Angela Buccieri raised her voice in mock incredulity and shook her head at Tommy Sciavoni, a nine-year-old multiple-fracture patient up to his sweet baby face in plaster of Paris. "You must think I'm dumb or something. Two all-time greats for one flash in the pan?"

Tommy smiled, enjoying the game. "Look, Doc, you're all hung up on these old guys. I mean, they were great, but they were *then*. The action is *now*, you know what I mean?"

Angela looked up and saw Dave Williams' large form entering the ward from the far end. "No way, Capone. I'll see you later. And in the meantime, you try and mend. Both your bones *and* your pirate ways, you hear." She rumpled his hair playfully and then walked over to greet Dave.

"Hi. Sorry I'm late."

"That's okay," Angela said. "How's it going?"

Dave gave the news reluctantly. "I think I'd better close up shop on the Harper matter."

Angela exploded. "Why?" Young heads on pillows turned in her direction.

"There's nothing to go on," Dave said softly.

"Are you kidding me?" She dropped her voice to a barely controlled hiss. "You and I both know Rowena Harper got so mad at a three-year-old child that she twisted her arm until she broke it. If she's done it once, she'll do it again. We have to stop her before she gets to that point. There should be a hearing on this matter."

44

"On what evidence? She cops to nothing. Her husband cops to nothing, not even his parenthood. Her attitude toward me was open, cooperative; the home is spotless; the child is spotless, no record of any previous problem. So you tell me what evidence?"

"I don't know—*find it!* Talk to friends. Talk to neighbors. *Someone* must have heard the kid screaming. St. Luke's Hospital across town—check the medical records there."

Dave found it hard to believe what he was hearing. It was suggestions like that which had finished Richard Nixon. He had thought Dr. Buccieri was mainly interested in the welfare of the child, from a professional standpoint. But he could see now that it went much deeper. She had a personal stake in this. "Easy, Doctor. Medical records are confidential, you know. Hers. Ours. Everyone's. I can't run around opening medical files and asking a lot of questions on the basis of a suspicion."

"You know—"

"And that's what it is, isn't it? A suspicion. There are other ways she could have broken that arm."

Angela took the six-foot-plus social worker by the arm and escorted him silently out of the ward. Around the corner was a storeroom stacked high with sterile bandages and linens. She led him in and closed the door.

"You know that baby did not break her arm falling out of that crib." Her tone of voice clearly indicated "off the record."

"Yes. I know that. But I don't know how she *did* break it. . . . And I don't know who else might have been involved. I cannot go from door to door putting an individual or a family under a cloud of doubt because of a hunch. Not only is that unprofessional, but it is against our Constitution."

Angela's hand impacted against the door with surprising force. "Up your Constitution, Williams! What about Mary Jane Harper? Who's looking out for *her* constitutional rights?"

Now Dave lost his temper. If he had been the door-pounding sort, the door would have been shattered. "Well, *I* am, for one, Buccieri! At least, I'm trying!" He paused and lowered his voice. "Wow, lady, you sure get angry."

"Yeah, I'm angry."

"And at the *wrong* people."

Angela took a deep breath and closed her eyes briefly. "When I was a kid in school and I missed a question, the nuns used to smack me across the knuckles with the sharp edge of the ruler. And when I ate too much at home, my father would knock me across the room. I grew up in halls that stank of garbage, with rats and cockroaches for pets, with rape around every

46

corner and the fear of punishment for breakfast every day."

Dave's sensitive eyes watched her as she spilled her guts. He could hear it coming, the thing that was driving her, coming straight out of the heart. "And you know what?" Angela asked him. "Your clean houses here may be filled with plastic flowers and the streets may be lined with palm trees, but it is no different. The anger and the hate and the frustration are here, and the kids are the victims, just like always."

She pointed out through the closet wall in the direction of the pediatrics wards. "I want to stay angry, so that as long as I'm alive, no kid *I* meet will ever think dying might be nicer than living . . . the way I did."

Dave was nodding his head. Her little history lesson had affected him. It seemed their attitudes were not very different. "Okay, tiger, I'll do a follow-up. Okay?"

Dr. Buccieri's muscles relaxed, and she gave Dave a grateful look. "Okay." She opened the door for him. "How do you stay so calm all the time?"

"Never had much to get mad at in my life." He knew the reason. "I was one of the lucky ones. My parents liked me."

Monday morning at ten o'clock Maria Val-

47

dez stepped off the bus at the corner and walked half a block to the Harper house. Of the four houses she cared for, she dreaded this one the most, particularly on Monday. When she did the Harper place on Thursday, it was an easier job; somehow the weekends brought out Mrs. Harper's messiest instincts. Sure enough, when she opened the door with her key, she was treated to a disgusting litter of bottles, boxes, and ashtrays. Everything seemed to be either half full or half empty. A couple of half-eaten pizzas decorated the coffee table, and several half-finished fifth bottles of liquor were distributed around the room. One of them had lost its cap and spilled on the carpet. Fortunately it was vodka—no stains to scrub.

She turned off the buzzing, forgotten television, cleared off the sofa, and began to clean it with a vacuum-cleaner attachment. The sound woke up the Harpers' child, who immediately began crying for her mother. Crying was all that baby knew how to do. But that was not her problem. Her job was hard enough.

At the same time the sounds of the house waking up began to penetrate through the multiple layers of gauze which were Rowena's head. Some guy had been over. But he wasn't Bill. They were never Bill. She didn't remember the rest. Her hangover was in full throb.

"Mommy? Mommy?"

Mommy, Mommy. Always Mommy. Endless demands. Unceasing. Mary Jane's howling became more insistent as Rowena felt the surface of the night table for a cigarette and lit one. The first blast of smoke grabbed her by the ears and pushed in with painful tightness.

"Mommy?"

"Maria?" Rowena shouted, but then realized Maria was vacuuming and couldn't hear.

"All *right!*" She stubbed out the cigarette and dragged herself across the hall to Mary Jane's room. It was the same old problem, the one which Mary Jane could never seem to master. Would she ever? Would it always be like this? "You wet yourself, and then you cry. Why don't you even *try* to go to the bathroom? Mary Jane? Stop crying. Please, Mary Jane, my head hurts."

A few minutes later Mary Jane was dry but still sniffling as Rowena led her by the hand into the kitchen. Mary Jane had a Tootsie Roll pop stuck in her tiny mouth—the all-purpose child quieter. As Maria put away the vacuum cleaner and began to dust, Rowena sat her child down at her little table. Now to find some breakfast for this kid. Rowena looked at the mountains of dishes in the sink and the crusty bowls and pans all over the kitchen counter. God damn it, where do they all come from? There's no end to the dishes, to the jobs around this house.

Christ, they'd had pizza delivered both Saturday and Sunday night, so where. . . .

Never mind. Here was some ready-made cereal; just add hot water and it's food. Rowena located the small bowl she used for Mary Jane's cereal. There was a little old stuff left over from yesterday morning, but it was all the same stuff. No problem. She ran the tap until the water was reasonably hot. It seemed to get less hot every month they owned this house. More than anything she wanted Mary Jane back in her crib and herself back in bed with a couple of aspirin massaging her brain.

"Okay, let's see the big girl feed herself."

Mary Jane screwed up her nose at the bowl and threw down her spoon. It clanged against the metal table, sending a shudder through Rowena.

"No!" the little girl said defiantly.

"All right. Mommy will feed you." She directed a spoonful toward the tiny mouth, but Mary Jane turned her head away.

"No. Don't like cereal."

"Well, that's all there is, and you have to eat it!" Rowena pinched Mary Jane's face around to face her and stuffed a spoonful of the oatmeal in her mouth. "If you don't stop squirming. . . ."

Mary Jane spit the gray goo right out at her mother's face. Fire flashed in front of Rowena's brain. She pulled her hand back and slapped Mary Jane hard across the mouth.

The sound of the slap caused Maria to turn her head. The child was wailing again, in pain. "I'm sorry, Mary Jane, I . . . I didn't mean to . . . . Oh, Maria." Mrs. Harper looked like a ghost as she skittered out of the kitchen. She was trembling all over. "Will you watch her, please? Please. I have to get out of here. I can't take it."

Rowena started toward her bedroom. "I can't. I can't take it."

The sun first passed through the leafy elms of the backyard. Then it filtered through the strands of ivy which swathed the mansion and finally through large diamond-shaped panes of thick glass. By the time it reached the circular table in the garden room of the Atherton home it was a pleasant mottled golden-green diamond pattern. The silver service set for breakfast was enhanced by this effect. Mrs. Atherton herself had designed the windows for the garden room, and it was her favorite place.

Thomas J. Atherton was a large man with an open, hearty face. His wife was somewhat of a contrast, tall, slender, very elegant. They seldom spoke over breakfast, and this morning was no exception. Thomas J. was immersed in his section of the paper, the financial news and sports, while Mrs. Atherton doted on the social pages and the advertising inserts.

Their routine was interrupted by the sound of a car in the nearby driveway. A few seconds later daughter Rowena was trudging up the flagstone steps to the garden room. Thomas J. leaped up from his chair to open the door for his little girl. Mrs. Atherton put down her section of the paper and pursed her lips a little tighter as she mentally prepared herself to be civil, knowing that it wasn't going to work.

"Rowena! Come on in, baby, have some breakfast."

"How is Mary Jane?" Mrs. Atherton asked in a cool tone.

"Oh, just fine. Her cast will be off soon."

"Don't you brush your hair anymore?"

Thomas J. waved "hush" at his wife while smiling at his daughter. "Stop picking on her, Laura. She just got here. Come and sit down, honey."

Rowena fell into an empty chair in front of the silver coffee urn. Her father leaned over his knees to pat his girl's hands. "How's the maid working out? She keeping things up for you?"

"Yes, thank you, Daddy."

Rowena's mother could not endure another one of these "how's-my-little-girl" scenes. She stood up from the table with a grace which showed her great concern for bearing. "Maybe," she said softly, but acidly, "you could find someone to go over there in the morning and brush her hair for her, Tom—she looks like a ragpicker." She gathered up her ration of the newspaper and left the room.

"That woman could cut diamonds with her tongue." Thomas J. chuckled at his own joke and then held out his arms to Rowena. "Come here, little girl. Tell Daddy what's wrong."

Rowena hesitated, but just a second. She really wanted a protected, little-girl feeling right now. And she always felt that way when she was sitting on her father's lap with her head against the broad front of his shoulder.

"I'm so tired. I wish I *was* a little girl again."

Thomas J. was a great believer in bucking up and the positive attitude. Things were never as bad as they seemed, particularly for Rowena, who could always rely on him. "Oh, well, don't worry," he began, bouncing her slightly on his knee. "Everyone has a bad day now and then. Your mother did everything but ride around on a broom when you were small. And you turned out okay."

"I'm not okay."

"Sure you are." He straightened her up and brushed her hair with his hand, as if his touch could take away the hurt. He saw in her face, however, that this kind of faith healing wasn't going to give him that "Oh, Daddy" smile this morning. Something more was needed. "Listen, I tell you what. What you need is a vacation. Maybe a cruise in the Florida Keys. Just Daddy and Rowena like in the old days. Remember—Crab Key and the beach you found there? Rowena Beach. Let's go back and discover it all over again. How does that sound?"

Thomas J. was surprised when Rowena abruptly stood up from his lap and turned her head away. Her voice was quavering. "Daddy, I'm scared. Someone from the hospital must have called the county because they sent a man to check up on me."

"What?" Thomas J. managed to hear *that*.

"This man came. He looked in her room and everything. I mean, like I had done something wrong, you know." Her father's face was scarlet with rage. "He was really nice, but I could tell what was on his mind. He thought—"

Thomas J. sprang to his feet and swiftly crossed the room. On a mahogany sideboard sat one of his most potent weapons—the telephone. He punched the digits with all the authority he could muster.

"Don't you worry about a thing. I'll handle this."

"I . . . I *want* to talk to someone, Daddy. I'm confused."

"Rowena," he told her sharply, "I told you I'd take care of. . . . Hello, get me Orrin Helgerson. Thomas J. Atherton calling. . . . Well, find him!"

There had been few rules between Rowena and her father. He had given her everything and asked for little in return. But one rule was inviolable—Daddy pulls the strings, and when Daddy is on the phone. . . .

Rowena departed down the flagstone driveway to her car. From the garden room she could hear her father's commanding voice chewing up the phone lines.

# CHAPTER

## IV

Angela was making some headway with at least one person at Santa Carla General Hospital—Tommy Sciavoni. His tough-guy act was beginning to waver that Saturday morning. He had offered an even trade—Ron Cey for Roger Maris. But, he'd warned the doctor such an uneven swap would surely affect his "will to live." The kids are getting too smart for me these days, Angela thought, as she handed over both Maris and Mantle. Too much television.

She just stepped out into the corridor when she nearly collided with Dr. Helgerson coming in. "Dr. Buccieri," he said flatly, then motioned for her to follow him. When they reached his office, there was no beating around the bush.

"You were ordered to drop the Rowena Harper matter. You disobeyed that order. As a result, Mrs. Harper's father, Thomas J. Atherton, who happens to be a trustee of this hospital, is threatening to *sue* this hospital." Helgerson was being very calm about it all, Angela thought. But there was a certain implied menace in his straightforward reporting of the facts.

But she knew where she stood and was not prepared to back away. "Thomas J. Atherton can go jump in the lake. He can't sue because the law in every state in this country says that any doctor who suspects child abuse must report it. As a matter of fact, I could be sued for malpractice if I didn't report it. So could you. And you know it."

There was no response from Helgerson. He simply rocked in his high-backed chair, studying Dr. Buccieri as if she were a player about to be selected for a sandlot baseball game.

"Furthermore," Angela continued. . . . And why not? she thought—bring a little light to the Dark Ages. "Furthermore, there are several state legislatures now considering bills which would indemnify and keep anonymous *any* citizen, doctor or no, who reports a case of suspected child abuse. I don't know about you, but I've always considered my medical degrees a kind of obligation to set an example."

Helgerson finally broke the silence. "I'm sorry

to tell you this, Doctor, but I am recommending to the board that since you have not lived up to the terms of your contract, it be terminated in the spring."

Angela was genuinely shocked. She had not expected that. She had had her differences of opinion with Dr. Helgerson, but she had always considered him a top-flight pediatrician and certainly never thought him some kind of martinet whose strings were pulled from the boardroom. She wanted to stay at Santa Carla General. It had one of the best pediatrics departments in the country. She could learn techniques here that were rare in most big cities. It was inconceivable to her that she might be fired for stepping on toes.

"You're gonna can me? Because of this?"

"Because of your general attitude. You are hostile, abrasive, and uncooperative. We are like a family here, Buccieri. To work well, we have to feel comfortable with each other."

"Yeah," Angela said halfheartedly. Sure enough, that was it—mashed toes. "Well, you can take the kid out of the ghetto, but you can't take the ghetto out of the kid. I should never have come uptown."

"Why did you apply here?" Helgerson asked. There was the suggestion of real curiosity in his voice.

"Why did you accept me?"

"As I recall, it was because you were at the top of your class."

Angela was on her way out. "Guess we were both disappointed. I came because I heard that this hospital practiced good medicine."

Angela felt hollow. It was a sensation she had rarely experienced. Generally there was enough anger or drive to fill her up, even on bleak days. But most of that seemed gone right now. Her chosen profession had let her down.

And she thought about Mary Jane Harper. What happens to her now? She knew she was right about Rowena, but. . . . Damn it, Buccieri . . . maybe if you'd taken it a little slower, been a little sweeter. Maybe if. Maybe if. . . .

It was a brilliant sunny day in Pioneer Park, a large city facility near the center of Santa Carla. Rowena and Mary Jane Harper strolled together across the broad expanses of lawn toward the children's play area. Mary Jane hadn't been to the park with her mother in several weeks. Rowena felt good to be there with her child today. Good to see Mary Jane's large black eyes wide with delight as she threw scraps of popcorn to the pigeons.

Rowena stopped briefly by the large monument in the center mall of the park. It was a somewhat grotesque iron statue of a pioneer family, a mother and father, a teenage son and a little girl. The jagged swirls of iron casting suggested crude clothes, and the deeply chiseled faces had eyes which peered dramatically into the future, over the far horizon to better grazing land. Rowena always found this thing ugly and embarrassing. Mostly because it was so important to her parents. Below the statue, on the marble pedestal which supported its ungainly collection of iron feet, were the "Rolls of the Pioneers," a listing of the first hundred settlers in the area. First on the list was "ATHERTON, AMOS." She remembered the day this clump of iron was uncovered and the splendid speech her daddy had given from the makeshift speakers' platform. "To the unending spirit of adventure and of life improvement, we dedicate this monument. Not to the handful of men and women whose names are recorded here, but to the living chain of pride which all Santa Carlans feel and to the secure, but never complacent, future of this fine city."

Rowena had been ten years old that day—how rotten of them to hold the ceremony on her birthday. She could still recall how she looked, her blond hair long and soft, wearing a pretty dress of yellow silk and a white corsage on her wrist. No birthday party. No kids her own age. Just the faces of the bored people staring up at her. Thomas J. Atherton's little symbol.

She pulled Mary Jane quickly by the statue:

"Swing, Mommy." Her bright little eyes had spied the swing sets nearby.

"Okay," Rowena said sharply, and tugged her toward the play area. It was her hurt. Her pain. None of it was Mary Jane's fault. It was so hard to remember that. She and Mary Jane were not the same person, and whatever she had done, it was not Mary Jane's fault.

Mary Jane struggled into a swing with her good arm and looked around for Rowena. "Push me, Mommy. Push me!"

"Okay, but hold on tight."

There was a mother pushing her little boy on the swing next to Mary Jane's. She looked over at Rowena and smiled. Rowena tried to smile back. Her expression was intended to convey some kind of . . . subconscious sorority of motherhood. I see you've got a child. This is mine. Aren't they wonderful?

The woman nodded toward Mary Jane. "Poor little thing, what happened to her?"

"She was chasing her kitten, and she fell down the stairs," Rowena said.

"Push me, Mommy. Push me!"

Rowena applied her palms to Mary Jane's back and sent the child upward in a long arc.

"She's a beautiful child," the woman continued.

"Thank you. She's her daddy's pride and joy."

"I can imagine. Look at that lovely dark hair. I bet she could do commercials if you wanted her to."

"Oh, her daddy would never allow that. He's very strict with her."

"She must be your first. He'll ease up after you have a couple more, believe me."

Rowena nodded, liking the game. Everything was fine. Bill would be back. Maybe tomorrow. And they would have more children. Everything would surely be all right tomorrow. Rowena found the rhythm of the swing and pushed Mary Jane higher and higher. She felt a sudden empathy with her little girl—how nice it must be to be three and at the end of a playground swing.

"Goddamn it!"

Rowena turned and saw a thin man in a cheap shirt walking nearby with a little boy. The boy had ice cream dripping down his arm and a smear of it all over his lower face. The man was furious.

"I *told* you to keep the paper napkin around that ice-cream cone. Now it's dripped all over you." He wrested the half-finished cone from the boy and bodily dragged him toward a water fountain. "Come here," the man snarled.

"Damn it, come here and get your hands clean, or you'll get it all over the car."

The woman next to Rowena lowered her voice to a confidential hush. "Isn't that disgusting? I tell you there are some people who are no more fit to be parents than animals."

Rowena felt her pulse quicken. They were on to her. Everyone in this park saw right through her. They knew what a lousy, terrible person she was. Just as Mommy knew. . . .

"You have to get a license to drive a car," the woman continued. "I don't see why you shouldn't be licensed to raise a child!"

"What?" Rowena said. "Why *I* shouldn't?"

The woman laughed. "Oh, honey, I didn't mean *you*. I meant the collective you. You know. 'One' I guess I should have—"

Rowena grabbed Mary Jane as the swing came back and held it motionless. "Mommy, push," the little girl said.

Rowena's voice trembled. "You said *I* should be licensed to raise a child!"

The woman's smile faded, and her eyes narrowed on Rowena as she removed Mary Jane from the swing. "Really, I didn't mean it personally."

"I haven't done anything." Rowena's voice quavered. Don't admit. They only think they know. Don't give them the satisfaction.

"Well, of course, you haven't—"

Rowena grabbed Mary Jane's unwilling hand and pulled her away from the playground. With the most prideful voice she could dredge up she announced, "Excuse me. My husband's waiting for us."

"Walk faster," Rowena hissed at Mary Jane as they returned in the direction they had come. The iron likeness of old Amos Atherton kept his eyes locked on distant horizons.

# CHAPTER

---

# V

It was nearing five o'clock at the Children's Protective Services office, and Dave Williams was preparing to make a fast getaway. He usually stayed until six each night, but he and Jeannie had tickets for the local dinner theater.

Just as it seemed possible that he might duck out on time this once, his phone rang.

"Dave Williams," he answered. "Yes, ma'am. ... No, you do not have to give me your name if you don't want to. ..." The woman on the other end mentioned a name which was familiar to Dave. He happened to have that case file on his desk, and he flipped it open. "Yes, we are looking into that. ... You did? ... No, ma'am, you will not have to appear in court, but if I could come down and talk to you—"

Then Dave was talking to a dead phone. Like so many others, neighbors, relatives, acquaintances, the woman had balked at the prospect of talking to someone official, of getting personally involved. "Thanks for calling," Dave said, and replaced the phone.

It was a typical experience for him. People were generally concerned where the welfare of a child was involved. But they tended to think of him as some kind of cop, possessing a cop's tendency to suspect everyone. Perhaps they feared he would come into their home for an interview, find something wrong with them, and forget the original purpose of the visit.

Some kind of cop, Dave thought to himself. Sometimes he wished he actually were a cop or, if not a real one, a television cop with clearly developed villains and no case lasting longer than an hour. As it was, his cases often dragged on for months, years sometimes, and involved a range of personal-encounter skills.

Dave had a Master of Social Welfare degree from the University of California. He was well grounded in sociology, but it was his courses and field experience in conducting interviews which served him the best and most often. Once the purpose of an investigative interview was announced to the parents, they generally clammed up. Getting the required information from them was like pulling teeth, but at least Dave knew what to look for. For example, there was the incredibly important family composition area. How many parents actually lived in the home? And if both were there, how did their relationship seem to be structured? Was one spouse always the boss? Sometimes it was easy to tell; other times Dave had to rely on nonverbal clues and intuition. He always felt a little shaky on this subjective ground. He recalled one interview, though, in which the husband and the wife had claimed to be equal partners. All during the interview the husband kept pulling lit cigarettes out of his wife's mouth and smoking them down himself. "That," Dave told the office staff later, "was the giveaway."

It was strange how the clues distributed themselves throughout his caseload. Despite what one might suspect, some of the most observable clues of child abuse occurred in families with "great expectations": the upwardly mobile young couples with children. They were so eager to impress and bring up children who were little models of themselves that they often went overboard. Dave recalled one such case in which the mother had developed the habit of simply latching onto the nape of her little boy's neck and "directing" him as they walked in public. The child behaved himself on this human leash even after a few cervical vertebrae cracked. Still, it was a routine school physical, not the mother, which detected the injury.

Simple parental ignorance often played a large role in abuse cases. Some parents simply did not know what to expect of a child and when to expect it. Often a child who was pushed to master toilet training too early would take longer to learn in the long run. When should the child begin to talk words? Or how about athletic prowess? How many children suffered because they were simply too young to master the feats expected by an athletic father? There were also more complicated areas of parental ignorance. It was essential for parents to establish a pattern of discipline for children and *stick to it*. The child had to feel that there was a consistent code for him or her to follow. Many parents, through either ignorance or apathy, failed to sit down together and establish such a code. The result was a confused child who was punished erratically. And often when those punishments did come, they were a release of pent-up parental frustration and resulted in injury.

Ignorance was sometimes compounded by pride. First of all, the parents were ignorant of the possibility that their child might be ill or congenitally weak. Hearing was the champion in this category, but there were many other weaknesses including some very common learning disabilities which were easily overcome with the proper schooling. Yet even when the possibility was pointed out to parents by a neighbor or concerned relative, their pride prevented them from investigating the matter with medical people. They felt such a weakness was a slur on them, and their pride was hurt.

Of course, not all cases involved such hidden motives. To be brutally honest, some parents were simply violent creatures who enjoyed hurting young ones or who did it under a cloud of alcohol or drugs. Dave had few illusions about human nature.

But far and away the most important point Dave sought to establish in his interviews was whether the parent had been abused as a child. The statistics were too clear to ignore on this matter—fully half of abusive parents had themselves been abused as children. That's what the books said; Dave suspected it was an even higher percentage. And if it was difficult to get a parent to talk openly to a social worker on the subject of toilet training or deafness, try budging them on their own history of abuse.

As for himself professionally, Dave considered one word the key: support. He had to be supportive. He had to always be there, an accepted presence in the family circle. He could be tough or gentle, just so long as he was *there* and the parents knew it.

Perhaps, he thought, it was time again to remind Mrs. Rowena Harper he was there. It had been more than a week since their last interview and he could drive past her place on the way to the theater.

He picked up the phone and punched the number of the nursery school where his wife worked. "Mrs. Williams, please. . . . Hi, honey? Don't yell, now, but I'm gonna be late. Why don't you get the sitter and go on without me? I'll meet you there. . . . Yeah, okay. . . . Coffee, lettuce, and toilet paper. See you later, babe."

He looked up to see his supervisor, Mrs. Ramish, standing in front of his desk—the feet of a cat that woman had. Ramish was a real pro, and he respected her. How she ran that madcap office was beyond human understanding.

"And don't forget the toilet paper," said the boss, smiling.

Dave launched into mock rhetoric. "I can handle everything about the new ways between men and women, *except* grocery shopping. *That* should be women's work."

Ramish was about fifty and white-haired, but she was as liberated as any coed. "Good luck, Charlie. Where're you going?"

"Follow-up on the Harper case, then home."

"Isn't that the one where you didn't find anything conclusive?"

Uh-oh. Dave heard it coming. The pressures of time and money were the worst features of work in public services. "Yes, but I think with a little more time—"

"Time we don't have. We've had a really heavy intake today, and Ramirez is out with the flu, probably for the rest of the—"

"Don't tell me that," Dave said, wincing.

"You got it, Dave. You'll have to make all her calls for the rest of the week."

Dave made a weary gesture toward his bulging file cabinet. "Mrs. Ramish, my caseload this month is forty-eight people."

"Close the file on Harper. That makes it forty-seven." Dave sighed his agreement and then accepted a memo his boss laid on his desk. "I want you to start work on this one right away, please," Mrs. Ramish continued. "The family's name is Mullin. Eagle Park area. The child is four years old. Severely burned. Just admitted to the hospital."

Dave glanced at the sheet. "Referred by the doctor?"

"Nope. Police department. There's a previous on file from last year. Second sheet." Ramish paused a moment while Dave studied the police report. "Someone must have heard that child screaming," she continued, shaking her head. "Why don't they report it?"

Dave stood and shoved the memo into his briefcase. "Getting involved means a hassle, man. Who needs it, right?"

Night had fallen in Santa Carla, and Rowena Harper hated to see it come. She remembered back to her high school days, when night meant excitement, dances, parties, escape from the house and her mother's continual faultfinding. It was under the blissful cover of night that she had first made love, to Charles Pederson, a senior, in her sophomore year, in his convertible along a deserted strip of highway. Night was wonderful when it signaled the end of an active day and the promise of a romantic night. Night was horrible when it meant another day had passed and nothing had happened.

Nothing.

And now it was night. The day was over. A single day out of her life down the drain. Just like a hundred other days spent in loneliness, isolation, with only a child for company.

I'm twenty-three goddamn years old. I'm young and good-looking, and I don't want to spend all my life like this, walking around the house all day, looking at the furniture my mother picked out and I hate.

Rowena poured herself another drink from the decanter. She felt disconnected. There were no reference points. Everything was blending.

Mary Jane whimpered softly in her room as Rowena put a record on the stereo. The music was soft and voluptuous. She moved to it, pretending she was dancing with someone, pretending someone who loved her was here.

She stubbed the cigarette out, half smoked, and poured herself another drink. On the table near the booze was a small white card. She picked it up and then recognized it: PARENTS ANONYMOUS.

The card sent a shiver through her spine, and she quickly replaced it. The drink burned as she gulped it down in two large swallows. Tears began to form in her eyes. That little child in there. Whimpering in her sleep, because of what. . . .

Because of. . . .

Because you can't control your impulses, that's why.

*No, don't worry. Everybody has a bad day once in a. . . .*

It *was* me. It was me who hurt her. The shadows stopped dancing. For a brief second the fog lifted, and she saw the picture clearly.

Rowena put down her drink and her cigarette and tiptoed out of the living room into the nursery. She looked at Mary Jane, so small, so vulnerable, her little face turned toward the back wall, whimpering softly.

"I'm sorry I hurt you," Rowena whispered to her sleeping child. Tears were rolling down her cheeks, unchecked. "I'm sorry. Oh, God! I hate myself so much."

She left the nursery door open and went into the living room. She found her old cigarette burned down to the filter and lit another.

What? Am I going crazy? she wondered. She paced, found herself in her bedroom looking at her old doll collection, and then she was out again in the living room. The silence was oppressive. Yet in the back of her mind she dreaded the thing which would break that silence. Not the doorbell. Not the telephone, with friends at the other end and a party building. No, Mary Jane was the sole source of sound in this house. And always, always the crying. Better the silence than that.

No, better the crying. . . .

"Someone talk to me. Can't stand this. I've got to talk to someone." She took a deep breath, dialed a number. "Hello," said Bill's voice.

"Bill? Hi. What're you doing?"

"Same old thing, Rowena. What's up?" He sounded hostile.

Rowena was desperate. "I . . . I thought I heard a prowler, and I got scared. Could you come over?"

"You sound ripped. You loaded?"

"No, Bill, I'm *not* drunk. I'm *lonely*. I want you to come home."

Bill's voice was cruel and to the point. "Don't tell me you're lonely. It's never been a problem for you. I bet you've got somebody—"

"Of course, I don't have a guy here. God, Bill, why do you always—"

"Rowena, I really can't talk now. I have a friend here."

Rowena felt hollow. She managed a civil sign-off. "Oh, so sorry. You should have said you had company."

She put the receiver down slowly, trembling. Always, always back to *that*. Bill Harper would never forget it and never forgive. It had been the biggest mistake of her life, that one night. She'd lost their first child in a miscarriage a few weeks earlier and had to get out of the house and away from Bill's eyes. Accusing, always accusing her. If she had taken better care of herself. . . . If she had stopped smoking and drinking. . . . If she had done some exercises as he'd suggested. . . . If she had listened to him. . . . If she had never run into that guy. . . . If she had never confessed to Bill. . . . If Mary Jane had not turned out to be such a nervous, whining child.

Rowena was wearing paths in the carpet from pacing. Twice, while recalling these things, she'd walked into the bedroom without even realizing it. Now she was standing at the small telephone table, searching through her address book for a card. There it was—PARENTS ANONYMOUS. An address near the university. She had to *talk* to somebody. Yes, she'd do it. Right now, before Daddy's voice told her again how right everything would be.

She put her cigarette down on the ashtray and went to find her coat. When she got in her car, she gave it a little too much gas on start-up and the machine roared in protest. She throttled back, drove into the street, and disappeared.

Mary Jane heard the roar of her mommy's engine in the middle of the night and stood up in her crib.

Her dark eyes grew large with fear when she couldn't see anything. She called for her mother, looking toward the door. There was little light coming from the living room.

"Mommy! Dark!"

There was no answer. She began to yell. "Dark! Mommy, come here. . . ." Her shouts quickly became screams when no Mommy appeared.

The Harpers' next-door neighbors, Brad and Nancy West, were getting ready for bed when Mary Jane's screaming began. They had noticed Rowena's car make its hasty departure, and now the familiar cries of the little girl were filling the neighborhood.

"She just drove off," said Mrs. West, concerned. "You don't suppose she left that child all alone, do you?"

"No. The maid is probably over there."

"But, Brad, listen to how she's screaming."

Brad West looked up from his toothbrush and shot a "mind-your-own-business" look at his wife. "Nancy, that child is *always* screaming. Close the drapes and just be thankful they don't have a dog."

It took exactly two minutes and forty-nine seconds for Rowena's 120 millimeter cigarette to burn halfway. Then the center of gravity shifted, and the cigarette tilted the other way, onto the tabletop. The filter came to rest on an open book of paper matches.

# CHAPTER

## VI

Judy Feinman was a small black-haired woman with a face that said, "I'm your friend." It was not always so. Judy had been deprived of her mother when she was thirteen. Her father had not wanted the responsibility of four children. He had not run off, as some had, though. He had stayed and hated staying. His children felt the brunt of his hate. Judy married early, still in high school. Her little girl was born soon after graduation. There was not enough money, not enough space, and not enough maturity for the young couple to cope.

One night, when her husband was out, Judy had beaten her two-year-old child so ruthlessly that the child had required hospitalization. This all happened back in Boston, where all the hospitals had well-organized Suspected Child Abuse or Neglect teams. SCAN for short. The doctor reported it immediately. Soon after Judy's husband split. Judy rapidly recovered from her initial feeling of revulsion about herself to realize that child abuse was not some evil deviation but rather a psychological unbalance which could be successfully treated. She went into treatment, relinquished custody of her child, and went back to school.

During her days of trouble Judy had become aware of Parents Anonymous. It was a nationwide organization, loosely tying together more than six hundred groups, encounter types of meetings in which troubled parents could find help. Or, more accurately, where they could find forums for self-help. There were Parents Anonymous groups in every state, in many of the major overseas U.S. military bases, and in several prisons. When Judy got a job in Santa Carla, she joined the local PA group. She was a frequent contributor to the quarterly PA newsletter.

Her current group consisted of six members. Some of them were still working out their first acknowledgment of the problem. Others were veterans who were stable enough to help newcomers and who still wanted the comforting atmosphere of people sharing the same feelings. The group roughly reflected human generations: Judy was the "grandmother figure," the solid base of experience and wisdom who was called on only when the "parent figures," the older group members, faced a particularly difficult problem. The "children figures" were the confused and frightened newcomers. Judy disliked neat analogies like this, but in the day-to-day business of the group, it actually seemed to work that way. The "children" were eager for love and acceptance, and the "parents" provided it.

Joy, one of the newer members of the group, was just beginning to talk when there was a timid rap at Judy's apartment door. Judy opened the door to reveal a very classy young woman in an expensive coat with long blond hair cascading down to the collar. Judy tried to make her feel at home. "Hi. I'm Judy. Welcome to Parents Anonymous."

"Hi," the woman said hesitantly, flourishing a small white card. "Uh, Mr. Williams gave me your card."

"Dave Williams is a good man. Glad you could come. What's your first name?"

"Rowena."

Judy led Rowena into the group and found

her a chair. "Excuse me, Joy. . . . Everyone, this is Rowena. Rowena, this is Joy, Margo, Hy, Sarah, Billie Rae, Sam, and Diana. Please sit down, Rowena."

Rowena sat as the group murmured hellos to her. She was instantly uncomfortable. She wanted to leave at that moment, but Judy smiled to relieve her uneasiness. Besides, one of the women was speaking, and Rowena didn't want to be rude. She'd make some excuse when the woman was done and leave.

The woman's name was Joy, and her voice carried the sharp twang of Oklahoma or Texas. "Like I was saying, thing is, I'd always jab Tommy with a fork to correct him. You know? If he was messin' up or something, and I was in the kitchen, which I just *always* was, I'd just jab him, like, 'Hey, you, watch it,' you know?"

Joy was sitting next to Rowena, and she jabbed an imaginary fork in Rowena's direction for emphasis. It wasn't an intentional gesture of hostility, but Rowena flinched just the same. Judy noticed it. She could tell that Joy was upsetting her. Well, that was normal. No one liked the company of people who shared one's deepest secrets. Not at first, anyway.

"I didn't mean nothing by it, really," Joy continued, her voice catching here and there, "least I really didn't think I did, until one day he made a mess on the floor. I'd spent all day cleaning . . . and—"

Joy broke down. The group said nothing. Rowena wondered what was coming now—a big group grope on the floor where everybody touched everybody and muttered, "I love you"? But they all just sat there, waiting for Joy to get her voice back.

"And I had this beer-can opener in my hand at the time. I didn't mean to hurt him so bad. Didn't even know I'd made a hole in him till he started bleeding."

Joy closed her eyes, too shaken to continue for the moment. A hole in him—Rowena shuddered. What kind of person was this? She could never imagine seeing Mary Jane's blood on the kitchen floor.

The shadows danced and showed her a woman putting out a cigarette on her child's naked buttocks. Viciously, purposely stabbing a lighted cigarette into the naked buttocks of a three-and-a-half-year-old child. Rowena blinked, and the shadows disappeared.

"I didn't know until I started coming here how angry I really was and how I was taking it out on him—like he stood for every rotten thing that ever happened to me in my life."

Judy was listening to Joy. But she'd heard

this story before and, without being obvious, was watching the new woman, Rowena. When Joy said "like he stood for every rotten thing," Judy was certain she saw a swift shudder go through Rowena. That was no new behavior for Judy. She'd seen it before. She called it the Shudder of Recognition.

It was Judy's policy not to comment unless the group reached a deadlock. The woman directly across the circle now took up the floor. She was Billie Rae, a "parent," the group member with the longest tenure. Billie had been coming for nearly three years. Her own problem was as licked as they get, but Billie continued to come for the support and to lend her own experience to others. God bless her, Judy thought.

Billie Rae was a large woman in her forties with soft red hair and a lovely smile. "Most important thing, Joy," Billie began, "you found out you weren't the only one. Like me. When my kid didn't do things my way, I'd just get madder and madder, and then I'd bite him. Just like I used to do when I was a little kid. I'd feel so helpless, you know, and then I'd just bite him as hard as I could. Thing I'm proud of now isn't that I don't bite him anymore. I never should have done that. The thing I'm proud of now is that sometimes when I feel like that, I

83

*know* what's going on with me, and I can deal with it."

Bravo, Judy thought.

"I get away for a while, you know, or just call someone here and just talk it out." She paused and looked directly at Joy, who had been listening raptly. "And I'll never hurt my kid again."

A flare of burning phosphorus in a dark house. . . .

Mary Jane had finally cried herself to sleep, and the Harper house was silent except for a slight crackling sound in the living room. The brilliant white flame of matches ignited by a fallen cigarette faded to the dull yellow fire of burning paper.

Then the crackling fire of burning cellophane from an empty cigarette pack. Then the dripping fire of nylon curtains. Then the thick, smoky fire of wood.

At Judy's apartment Sam filled his cup with coffee from the big urn on the side table.

"Everyone hits their kid sometime, right? My father whipped me to get me into line, I can tell you that. I thought it was okay."

The group had broken up its pattern of personal stories for the moment and was shooting the breeze in an open format. Everyone was commenting at once.

"That's the same with me," the woman named Margo added.

"Yeah," said Hy, a short man in a suit, "except you really don't learn anything but more hate and more anger. And that's what you end up teaching *your* kids, and that's what they teach *their* kids, and it never stops."

Everyone added his agreement to this last statement; it seemed to sum up a lot of what they'd been saying. Rowena too saw the wisdom, or at least the accuracy, of what Hy was saying. She nodded her head ever so slightly.

A mistake, she realized immediately. Now they all were looking at her. God, I really can't do this, she thought. I'm a private person. I've never been able to. . . .

"Rowena," Judy said gently, "would you like to share with us tonight?"

Rowena squirmed on her chair and tried a ploy. "Oh, I'm a little embarrassed. You see, I never beat my kid or anything like that." She turned on all her charm. "She got hurt falling out of her crib. It was an accident."

The group sat in frozen silence. Then some of them began sharing knowing looks.

"The county sent this social worker to see me," Rowena continued. "That's how I happen to be here tonight. But it's all a mistake."

Judy said nothing. She'd let the group take care of this.

The group wasted no time. "Oh, man," Margo moaned. Another one of *those*.

She turned in her chair and angrily confronted Rowena. "Listen, you, I'm sitting here spilling my gut, and I'm doing it because this is a place where I can be honest. You want to play games, go to a schoolyard."

Hy was a little more understanding. "Tell it like it happened, kid. Hang it out there." He smiled at her benignly. "Your laundry's no dirtier than anyone else's."

Rowena was still frightened, but she looked from face to face around the group and saw that they were really sincere. Even Margo was less hostile than her voice made her sound.

Then Joy spoke again. Her soft eyes gave Rowena the impression that they had seen all the world had to offer and that they could see into her even now. "You've been drinking, haven't you, hon? Were you drinking the day your baby . . . had the accident?"

Rowena nodded. Judy's hand found hers and grasped it tightly as Rowena began to talk, slowly at first, shedding layers of resistance and disguise, telling her story.

"Mommy!"
"Mommy!"

The child's voice resonated with mortal fear. The living room was dark no longer; ever-increasing jets of white smoke were pouring into the yellow nursery, and behind the entering smoke was a dull red glow. It was getting hot in the nursery, and Mary Jane sensed the danger as readily as she tasted the acrid smoke in her nostrils.

Where was her mommy?

"Mommy!"

Rowena Harper was crying and clutching Judy's palm as if it were the rescuing hand of a mountaineer. She was trying her best to tell about Mary Jane. But somehow—why—the tale always came back to someone else.

"I had to hurt her to make her *listen* to me," Rowena sobbed.

"Your kid?" Judy asked.

"My mother," Rowena answered, not really knowing what she was saying. "She wouldn't *listen* to me. Mary Jane is just like her. She looks like her. She hates me. She spoiled things between Bill and me."

Something else was bothering her now, though. Something she had just said. What was it?

"My mother said I was bad. She said . . . I did bad things with my father. But I didn't! Mary Jane is—"

Mary Jane is home in the house all alone! My God!

Rowena was on her feet, swiftly gathering up her purse and coat. "Listen . . . I shouldn't be here now . . . I wasn't thinking . . . I have to get home." She started for the door.

"Call us anytime you need help, Rowena. Every Tuesday night we're here. We're in the book."

Rowena was gone. The group looked at each other, trying to assess what they'd just heard. Judy was actually a little amazed. The young woman had wandered in, had resisted, but had ended the evening by giving more of herself than most do on the first meeting. There was definite hope for Rowena.

Rowena drove at high speed all the way home.

The first thing she noticed was the corner near her house. It was slick with water! Her car slid around the turn, and she just managed to avoid slamming into a parked car. What was going on?

Then she saw the source of the water. It was gushing down the street from fire engines parked in front of her house.

"Oh, God!"

She ignored the cop controlling traffic, and

the car bounced madly over the maze of thick fire hoses that were snaking all over the street. She jumped from the car and ran toward the house, eerie in the sweep of red fire-engine flashers. Three trucks . . . smoke wafting out the front door . . . Brad and Nancy West in bedclothes . . . a police officer on the front walkway. . . .

"My baby! My baby's in there," Rowena screamed.

The officer caught her by the arm and held her away from the house. "Are you Mrs. Harper?"

"Yes, oh, yes. What happened? Where's my baby?"

The officer released her arm and spoke softly, almost as if he wanted to keep the good news a secret. "We have her, Mrs. Harper. She's all right."

"Thank God. Where is she?"

"We took her to the hospital to check for smoke inhalation. You were lucky, Mrs. Harper. The fire was localized to your front room." He nodded toward the Wests. "Your neighbors spotted it in time."

"I want to see Mary Jane."

"Not right now, ma'am. Leaving a small child alone in a house is not only dangerous, but against the law."

The officer gestured toward the open rear door of his squad car. "I'm afraid you'll have to come with me."

# CHAPTER

# VII

"Hey, Buccieri."

Angela was off duty and about to catch the elevator to the ground floor when she heard her name announced to the whole floor. She turned to see Dr. Mark Handelman approaching. Mark was a resident in internal medicine at Santa Carla. They had met at a few parties and hospital functions.

"Young Dr. Handelman, I believe," Angela announced back at him as if she were the narrator of a daytime soap opera.

"The heart beats faster. She remembers me."

Mark was tall and thin and always seemed to be formulating some kind of witticism. "What can I do for you, Mark?" Angela asked.

"Have a drink with me and hold my hand."

Well, that was a surprise! "The heart beats faster. I thought you dated only little blond nurses."

"I've changed my style. Now I go for little dark doctors."

"Are you sure you're not weird?"

"No. I've decided you're very cute."

Well, all right, Angela thought. Mark was kind of cute himself. "I'm gonna wire my mother right now," Angela said with make-believe breathlessness.

Mark grinned. "Tell her I may even take you to dinner."

The elevator opened behind them, and the two young doctors waited for it to clear. One patient caught Angela's eye—she was a small female child with a cast on her right arm. She hustled back onto the pediatrics floor to catch up with the injured child.

"Hold it!" she cried, and she looked at the little face beneath an oxygen mask.

"Son of a bitch. . . ."

She felt a long string of juicy Italian curses dancing on her tongue, but she bit them back and turned to the police officer who was accompanying Mary Jane Harper.

"What happened?"

"The mother left her alone, and the house almost burned down," the officer said. The gurney and orderlies continued down the hallway.

"Mark, this love affair's gonna have to be continued another night." She tried to sound apologetic.

"You know the kid?"

"I've treated her before." Angela sighed. "Later, huh, Mark?"

"I'll hang around," Mark offered.

Angela nodded. Then she walked to the nurses' station and without hesitation picked up the phone.

Dr. Helgerson's service provided a number—his home.

"This is Dr. Helgerson."

Angie could hear the sounds of a quiet dinner party.

"Dr. Helgerson? Angela Buccieri. Guess what your good friend Atherton's little girl did this time?"

Angela entered Mary Jane's room. She felt her heart sink.

The little girl was lying motionless on the large bed. She looked so alone beneath the crackling plastic of the oxygen tent which surrounded the upper half of the bed. How frightened the child must be, isolated from the world, with no place of safe refuge, not even her own room at home.

She slowly approached the bed and sat on a tiny corner of it. She had stopped in the children's dayroom and picked up a doll. It was not a "baby" doll but rather had long dark hair, a tiny dress, and high-heeled shoes. It was one of the dolls the psychiatric staff used in play therapy. It represented "Mommy."

"Had yourself a scary time, huh?" Angela began gently as she applied her stethoscope to Mary Jane's chest. But Mary Jane was wearing the Mask. "Don't want to talk?"

The child simply stared at her. Angela screwed her face into a hurt expression, which wasn't very difficult. "Are you mad at me?"

Almost imperceptibly Mary Jane Harper shook her head no. Okay, Angela thought, at least she's got her ears open. The trauma hasn't driven her totally into herself.

"That's good. Because I've taken quite a shine to you, kid, and there's nothing I would like better than to be your friend." She produced the doll and curled back the oxygen tent so that Mary Jane could see it better.

"Do you like dolls?" Mary Jane nodded slightly. "Me, too," Angela continued, now hushing her voice to the here's-a-secret tone children loved. "I'm gonna tell you a secret. My mommy and daddy weren't very nice to me when I was little. So I used to pretend my dolly was my mommy. At night, when the lights were out and everyone was gone, I . . . I would talk with her."

Angela felt her throat begin to ache as she looked into Mary Jane's eyes, looking at her from behind the Mask. Those jet-black eyes, which had seen most of the cruelty and pain in the world in the short years they'd been collecting light.

"I used to ask her why she was so mean to me. Sometimes I told her I loved her, hoping she'd hear." Angela paused. "Mary Jane, how did your arm get broken?"

Mary Jane shut out the disturbing question. She pulled her knees up to the fetal position and turned away from the doctor.

"Okay," Angela continued, "you don't have to talk to me." She reached over and deposited the doll in Mary Jane's bed next to her. "You talk to her. Maybe she'll help."

Mary Jane slowly found the doll and pulled it close to her. Good, Angela thought, now's the time to leave them alone for a while. She'd leave instructions with the nurse on duty in the room to remember anything the child said to the mommy doll. And later she'd return and try to—

There was a loud crash.

The doll lay against the wall where Mary

Jane had thrown it with surprising force. The impact had shattered the doll's plastic face.

Angela sagged against the doorframe just outside Mary Jane's room and dabbed her eyes with the sleeve of her white jacket. In a few moments she sensed a flurry of activity at the nearby nurses' station. Dr. Helgerson had arrived, in dinner jacket and bow tie, and was issuing orders to the nurses.

"Call our respiratory therapist," Helgerson commanded. "And have the lab check the blood samples for oxygen tension."

"Yes, Doctor," said a nurse on the phone.

"Also notify radiology. I want a full set of skeletal X rays. Stat."

Angela pushed her shoulder blades away from the wall and crossed over to where Helgerson was holding court. "Aren't you off duty tonight, Doctor?" he asked her.

"I was. I stayed to see if I could be of some help."

Helgerson seemed to have mellowed toward her with the arrival of this fresh evidence of neglect. "You'll have the grace to spare me the 'I told you so's,' won't you?"

"Sure. May I ask you a question?"

"Yes."

Angela didn't feel like a fight. Her encounter with Mary Jane had left her drained. "Why don't we have a child abuse team at this hospital? Or even a social worker on the staff? Why isn't anyone here trained to prevent"—she nodded toward Mary Jane's room—"this?"

Helgerson told her the simple truth. "It was never thought necessary before."

When Helgerson entered Mary Jane's room for a personal examination, Angela walked over to Mark Handelman. Her voice was a little shaky and apologetic. "I've got to level with you, Dr. Handelman. If you want to boogie tonight, I'm afraid you have the wrong partner."

"I'm a very versatile guy," Mark said quickly but sympathetically. "I also know how to talk."

Angela leaned against his rangy frame. "Thank you."

Rowena Harper was still in a state of shock later that night when her father opened the massive oak door of their Tudor mansion.

She no longer thought or felt anything. She went where she was told.

"Don't they sometimes have reporters at police stations?" she heard her mother ask.

"Don't worry, Mrs. Atherton," said a voice. "I'll keep this out of the papers." It was Mr. Bernard, the lawyer.

Thomas J. stood next to Rowena while her

mother sat in a wingback chair across the room, lips pursed. "I just don't understand it," Thomas J. was saying. He laid his hand on Rowena's shoulder, but her attention was still attracted by the flames in the fireplace. "What happened to you, honey? If you had to go off, why didn't you call us? We could have sent someone over to watch Mary Jane."

"I don't know," Rowena muttered. "I just don't know."

Mr. Bernard cleared his throat. He was a *tall*, slick-looking man in his mid-thirties. "Look, let's deal with the realities here. Now we'll have to go to a prehearing in juvenile court within forty-eight hours. The judge will decide whether to let Mary Jane come home."

Thomas J. frowned. He didn't like this meddling procedure—a judge deciding who was to bring up his grandchild. His encounters with the law had always been connected with business and at a much higher level. He dreaded the thought of a municipal judge in a juvenile court.

But Mr. Bernard was confident. "I'll get her home, don't worry. The big hurdle will be the formal hearing in two weeks." He glanced at Rowena's silent, hunched-over form. "The first thing we do is get Rowena into treatment with a well-known psychiatrist."

"Absolutely," said Thomas J. "Get her the best. I don't care about the cost."

"The point is to get a man the court knows and sometimes consults."

Atherton nodded and then smiled at his lawyer. He could see the strategy developing. Mr. Bernard was worth his less-than-modest fee.

"Then we'll want letters," Mr. Bernard continued, "attesting to Rowena's good character. A clergyman is always good. And someone who has seen her with the baby."

"We'll get it done."

"Now, at the formal hearing, the doctor from the hospital may bring up the question of Mary Jane's broken arm. Mrs. Harper, were there any other injuries found the day she . . . had the accident?"

Rowena, lost in the flames, was vaguely aware of her name and a question directed at her. "Mrs. Harper?" the lawyer asked again.

She turned toward the man. "Any other injuries?" she asked in a barely audible voice, her face advertising remorse.

Oh, brother, thought Mr. Bernard, what a witness. Keep her off the stand at all cost. "From . . . any other accidents she might have had? Did they do any other X rays besides the arm?"

"No," Rowena muttered. "They wanted to

keep her, but I wouldn't let them." She paused, thinking back to that day in the hospital, wishing it were that day again. "I was wrong. I should have let them keep her."

There was a shocked silence in the room. "Rowena," Mr. Bernard warned, "don't ever say anything like that again."

"Do you want to know what really happened the day she broke her arm?" Rowena said swiftly, almost in a whisper. She was ready to tell them the whole story. God, she'd told it to a group of strangers earlier that night; why couldn't she get through this barrier to her own family, to her own daddy?

"No," Mr. Bernard insisted. "It does not matter."

"Why, Mr. Bernard?" Rowena raised her voice. "Why doesn't it matter?"

"Just answer the questions *I* ask you and do no other talking to anyone. Is that clear? . . . Now, where did you go tonight?"

Rowena bowed her head and retreated into herself again. "I felt like I was going crazy. I *was* going crazy. The social worker said there was a place to go where people like me talked to each other. . . . I went. It's called Parents Anonymous."

"You went where?" Thomas J. bellowed.

But the lawer waved him off. "Did you say

anything that could be used against you?" Mr. Bernard asked.

"I don't know," Rowena said meekly. "I don't remember." She knew her father and mother would never understand the value of the experience, but she felt like trying.

"Did you give your right name?"

"They just used first names."

"My God!" Mrs. Atherton said behind clenched teeth. "You went to a group of strangers? You told *those* people your personal business?"

"They listened to me." Rowena turned a pitiful face toward her parents. "They heard me. They understood. I want to go back!"

"Over my dead body," her mother announced. "Do you know what could happen if any of those people know who you are?"

Rowena turned her head back to the fireplace. "They do," she said.

Mary Jane Harper was the first customer when the morning shift hit the X ray room. She had priority—they had fewer than twenty-four hours to prepare a full X ray picture for the preliminary hearing.

An hour later a large packet of X rays labeled "Mary Jane Harper—Long Bones" lay on the table next to a wall of fluorescent X-ray viewing screens. Tom Greenberg, the radiologist, had just finished viewing a large stack of X rays from the day before and was about to start with Mary Jane's when his phone rang. He'd been waiting for this call.

"Yeah, Greenberg. . . . Well, Samuel, what did you think? A hell of a game and one hell of a hundred bucks you owe me. . . . Ha-ha. . . . I'll tell you, those Vikings remind me of a Marine platoon."

Just then, a clerk pushing a rolling file cabinet full of X ray packets entered the room.

"Hold on a minute," Greenberg said into the phone. "For the files?" he asked the clerk.

"Yes."

"It's the bunch on the left."

The clerk lifted the pile of manila envelopes, and they came sliding apart, cascading to the floor. As he knelt to pick them up, his left hand felt for the ones which had fallen back onto the desk. By mistake, his hand also latched onto Mary Jane's file.

He finally got them all arranged and stuffed into his cart. "My friend," Greenberg was saying into the phone as the clerk left the room, "my friend, if you say that, then you just don't understand the psychology of the game."

At four o'clock that afternoon Dr. Greenberg was on the phone again. "What do you mean it's not back yet?" Dr. Orrin Helgerson was saying. "They shot her this morning. I need a reading on that Harper X ray this afternoon. Call me as soon as you get them. It's vital, Tom. Vital."

# CHAPTER

## VIII

Dave Williams slid into a seat in the back
row of the juvenile courtroom of Santa Carla
County Courthouse. Dave had attended
hundreds of these prehearing sessions in his
time, but this one promised to be particularly
interesting. The Atherton name was well known
in the community, and he was curious to see
just how fine those slow wheels of justice were
going to grind today.

The clerk called, "Order! Order! Juvenile
Court of the County of Santa Carla in the City
of Santa Carla is now in session. Judge F. F.
Carlson presiding. All rise."

Carlson. Well, that was a good omen. Judge
Carlson was known to be a fair but strict man

who did not hesitate to act in such cases. He was a white-haired man of about fifty-five with a slight limp to his gait. When he was settled behind the bench, everyone in the courtroom sat again. Judge Carlson studied the brief before him for a moment, then began.

"Now then, I see the minor in question, Mary Jane Harper, received an injury six weeks ago. At that time a request was made for an investigation by the Children's Protective Services. . . .

"According to this report from CPS, the home is clean and the child well cared for. Suspicion of abuse not confirmed. The medical report. . . ." He looked for it in his pile of briefs, and Dave's ears perked up. "The medical report tells me that full skeletal X rays have been ordered, but not yet received."

Dave couldn't believe his ears. How could Angela let this happen?

"The hospitals are getting as bad as the mail service," the judge joked. Rowena's lawyer smiled, and Mr. Atherton chuckled aloud, eager to show the judge he was a *simpático* man of the world.

"And here," Judge Carlson continued, holding up a handful of letters on crisp letterhead stationery, "are some impressive letters of testimony to the excellence of your character, Mrs. Harper."

Rowena managed a charming smile. But the judge's attitude now changed, and he was not charmed at all. "Everything about you seems responsible, young lady, and yet you put your child's life in grave danger."

The change in attitude sent a shudder through Rowena. There was a short pause in the courtroom as the judge apparently wanted some explanation. Mrs. Atherton's coiffured head craned from side to side, as if looking for a fast way out.

Mr. Bernard was quickly on his feet.

"Your Honor, we are aware of the serious nature of the charge of child endangering. However, there are mitigating circumstances." He gestured toward Rowena, and his voice fell to a sympathetic, pleading tone. "This is a young woman who was deeply in love with her husband, the father of her child. His abandonment unsettled her mind, made her temporarily unstable. Mrs. Harper has volunteered to undergo psychiatric therapy, and her parents, Mr. and Mrs. Thomas J. Atherton, will assume the responsibility of supervision."

Atherton subtly raised his right hand when his name was mentioned, a gesture which Dave perceived as being more appropriate for an auction of antique cars than a child custody prehearing.

The lawyer's explanation and the supportive

presence of grandparents was enough to convince the judge, however. "This court finds that acceptable," he announced. "Custody of minor returned to her mother pending the formal hearing."

The hearing adjourned. Dave was not surprised at the outcome. Without the X rays it would be difficult to prove a history of abuse. And now, with the precedent of the prehearing, the prospects for the formal hearing were looking dimmer and dimmer.

Oh, brother, he thought, tonight's dinner is going to be a lulu.

"Returned custody?"

"Yep."

"I don't believe it!"

Angela Buccieri was smoking mad. She glared at Dave Williams as if waiting for the punch line to a cruel joke. There wasn't one.

Mark Handelman leaned against the mantelpiece of the Williams's living room, sipping a drink, watching his date imitate an overdue volcano. Angela had received the invitation to dinner at the Williamses' a few days ago and had invited him along. He was really beginning to enjoy the company of his volatile colleague. He liked the Williamses, too. Jeannie Williams appeared in the middle of the scene with a plate of guacamole dip and a big basket of taco chips. She deposited them on the coffee table and then looked from face to face.

"You had to bring it up before dinner, didn't you?" she asked her husband good-naturedly.

Angela was wearing an attractive denim jumpsuit with zippers everywhere. With her hands on her hips, she looked like a race driver who'd just been scrubbed from the Grand Prix. "I don't understand," she said. "That child has been so badly damaged that she's now mute. What about her broken arm? What about the fact that she could have been burned to death? What about the skeletal X rays? I heard Helgerson order them myself. What did they show?"

Dave plowed a furrow in the green dip and popped the chip into his mouth. "They weren't back yet," he explained casually. He wasn't being callous about the prehearing results. They had disappointed him as much as anyone. But it was clear that the doctor had too high an expectation of the power of the court and that she had only a vague idea of how these things worked. Frustration was a daily diet supplement for a social worker. Angela's fire was commendable, but it would burn itself out if he failed to bank the coals with a little reality.

"That's impossible," Angela answered. "It takes less than forty-eight hours."

"Unless, of course, some dingbat orderly

thought it was a new graphic and had it framed for somebody's office." Mark's attempt at humor gathered no laughs. "And in our place it could happen," he added.

"Well," Dave continued, "without the X rays, there was no damning evidence against Rowena Harper other than that she went out for an hour and left the kid sleeping in her crib."

Angela sounded momentarily defeated. "I could use another drink," she said.

While Dave mixed the new round, Jeannie set the table. The silence was broken by the sound of the Williams boys roughhousing in their room. "I knew it was too quiet around here," Jeannie said, smiling. "Be right back."

Dave handed the two doctors fresh drinks. "I'll tell you a little secret. In juvie the judges tend to make their decisions on the basis of how things look. You've seen Rowena Harper. She doesn't fit the profile of an abusive mother."

"What profile?" Angela challenged. "There isn't any profile. It's not just blacks, or Italians, or lower middle class, or red-necks, or welfare mothers. It's anybody . . . and everybody."

Dave shrugged. "I know. But try to get the public to believe it."

"So you're saying the judge is the general public, huh?"

"He's just a guy like anybody else. Besides,

there are other considerations. A three-year-old child *is* better off with her mother than in a foster care situation."

Angela couldn't accept that. "What are you saying? I've read the books. I've seen the statistics! One out of two severely beaten children dies after being returned to his parents. My God, Dave, child abuse is *the leading cause* of death for children under the age of five in this country. Why don't we just take the kids away from these monsters and keep them away?"

Dave was relaxed on the couch, but his hands were soaring in the air, casting about for some understanding from Angela. "Because we are not talking about monsters, Angie; we are talking about human beings. Some are psychotic, but most are not. Most abusing parents are dependent, frightened people reacting to pressures they don't understand and don't know how to handle. And most are reclaimable. Ninety percent, in fact."

Jeannie had returned to the living room during Dave's explanation. "He's right, hon," she added. "And take it from a working nursery-school teacher, small children don't want to be separated from their parents, even cruel and abusive ones."

Dave continued. "Good foster homes are scarce, and county institutions are overcrowded and sometimes more dangerous than the home."

Angie couldn't argue with the truth of what Dave and Jeannie were saying. "Then what do we do?" she asked.

"The best we can," Dave answered. But that was no answer. "I tell you what we need: We need a tight system of support for parents who are failing. We need hot lines in every city in every state in the country. We need groups like Parents Anonymous where people filled with shame and guilt can come and talk to one another and be understood. . . ."

Jeannie had her own favorite analogy for this situation. "If you ask me, we need the same kind of instant reporting of child abuse that people volunteer when they see animals being hurt. Can you imagine what would happen if you went outside right now and kicked a dog across the street? Drapes would fly open. Searchlights would sweep the neighborhood. The telephones would hum with protests. But when someone kicks a kid, no one says a word."

"And why?" Dave asked sardonically. "Because maybe that's the way the guy *trains* his kid. So we need to get to the parents in time. Children who are abused become abusing parents."

"Okay, Dave," Angela said finally, "I hear what you're saying. But surely *sometimes* the parent is too far gone to have a kid around? Surely sometimes a child has to be removed from the home?"

"Yeah. Sometimes."

Angela's memory fetched up the images of what she had seen in the hospital. The frightened look on Mary Jane Harper's face beneath the plastic of the oxygen tent. The Mask. The doll with its face shattered against the wall. "Well, I believe with all my heart that Mary Jane Harper is one of those. And I think, gut level, you do, too."

Dave had no response. He had his arm around his wife on the couch, and his eyes seemed intent on the swirls of guacamole.

"We've got two weeks, Dave. Let's prove it."

# CHAPTER

# IX

The next morning found Drs. Buccieri and Handelman working opposite ends of the same mystery.

Mark started his trackdown with Dr. Greenberg, to discover if he might have misplaced Mary Jane's file somehow. Together they explored every drawer and horizontal space in the radiology section. When they came up zero, Mark began hunting down orderlies and clerks.

Angie started at the other end—the X ray table. The operator remembered Mary Jane perfectly and was sure that X rays had been done. The technician who unloaded the plates also remembered the job. It had been high-priority, and he had carried Mary Jane's films to the lab in a separate trip rather than wait until he had a bunch, as was the routine procedure.

The chief lab technician failed to recall Mary Jane by name. But he assured Dr. Buccieri that they had been done and produced his logbook to prove it. "Mary Jane Harper" was clearly listed in the "Developed" column along with a number of negatives consistent with a full skeletal X ray.

At the same time, across town, Dave Williams was beginning his investigation at the source—the Harper home. He had determined when Rowena Harper would be out that afternoon at her psychiatrist's office. It was the other adult in the home to whom he wanted to talk.

"Please, *señor*. My English . . . *no está bien*." Maria, the maid, was studying him suspiciously across the transom. The language was a genuine problem for her, but she was no fool. She knew what was happening in the household and was not about to place her employers in a position where they might be forced to fire her.

Dave tried to persist. "Maria, you are here almost every day. I only want to know if you have ever seen Señora Harper hurt *la niña*." Dave bunched up a large fist and swung it down through the air. "Hurt. Hit. Scream at. You know what I'm asking."

But Maria's brown face was unflappable. "Señora Atherton pay me to come clean here. I

114

don't hear nothing. I don't see nothing. I just clean. You want to know something, you ask Señora Atherton. I don't know nothing. *Nada. Nada.*"

The door closed in Dave's face, and he started walking back to his car. "Go ask Mrs. Atherton," she had suggested. What was Maria suggesting? That Dave should talk to Rowena's mother for the real story?

He hadn't planned on talking to her so soon. He wanted to get some more background before interviewing the principals. But maybe now was the time to visit the mansion.

He waited a full thirty minutes in the foyer before a maid showed him into the garden room. The house was very impressive and loaded with fine paintings. Under different circumstances he would have been overjoyed to see original O'Keeffes and Wyeths. But he kept his enthusiasm to a minimum, for he knew Mrs. Atherton would be arriving any minute. When she finally did appear, she took a stance by the breakfast table and let the sun's green-and-gold diamonds cover her dress. "What can I do for you, Mr. Williams?" she said in the most formal voice she could muster.

Dave explained his position. He was not trying to incriminate anyone. His job was to provide the court with background information about the home and the mother. Mrs. Atherton nodded as if she understood. But when she spoke, it was as if Dave had just kicked in the door with a search warrant.

"We have a lawyer, Mr. Williams. I believe he is the one you should be talking to."

"Mrs. Atherton," Dave repeated, "I'm not the police. I'm not trying to punish anyone."

"Oh, really?" Mrs. Atherton responded coldly. "It was my impression that you represent the state and that the state feels my daughter is an unfit mother."

The woman made Dave feel cold. He was about to explain again, but he hesitated. Mrs. Atherton didn't seem to be there with him. It was as if the problem with Rowena were something she'd read about in a newspaper. And the way she'd spoken those last words—"an unfit mother." There was no outrage at the suggestion, almost as if *that* were a foregone conclusion. What she had insisted on making clear was that the "state" had no business in her home.

Dave took the plunge. "And what do you feel?"

Dave expected the woman to bristle, lash out at him, call the servant to show him out. It was obvious that her privacy was important to her.

But Mrs. Atherton did none of those things. She turned away from the room and stared out across the spreading lawn of the back yard.

Down to the curving back driveway. Down to a taxicab parked there, with its trunk open and bulging, and across the lawn strolled her husband, Tom, and little Rowena, hand in hand, off for a month in the Florida Keys without her. "Ahoy, little girl." She could still hear Tom's rasping, comic "pirate voice" and the delighted giggles of the child. Of his "little girl."

"I feel nothing," she said to the panes of cut glass. "I haven't felt anything for years. The two of them shut me out a long time ago." She glanced around at the social worker. "If Rowena is spoiled and selfish, it's his fault. Nothing was ever too good for Daddy's little angel."

She turned back to her ghosts. "Don't ask me about Rowena. I'm an outsider."

The X ray clerk's name was Carlos Sanchez, and he was surprised to find a pediatrics resident waiting for him by the men's room, where he changed his clothes prior to going on duty. The lady doctor was sweet but firm. She asked him a number of questions about his duties and the standard procedure for filing X rays. When she asked him about Dr. Greenberg and some missing X rays, he nodded slowly, remembering.

A few minutes later he was showing her the third-floor file room where the inactive medical records were stored. He applied his key to the locked door.

"It was about a week ago, Dr. Buccieri. I picked up the usual load of inactive files from radiology. Dr. Greenberg was on the phone, as I remember. He just pointed to a pile and told me to take 'em."

They entered the file room. Carlos swung a small ladder around and climbed up to check an oversized box on top of a cabinet.

"You said the name was Harper?" he asked as he flipped through the box.

"Mary Jane," replied an anxious Dr. Buccieri.

"Here she is." Carlos handed her a manila envelope with the words "Mary Jane Harper—Long Bones" clearly written in the data box.

"Thank you. Thank you, Carlos, very much."

Five minutes later she had snagged Dr. Helgerson from his rounds, and the two of them were walking swiftly toward radiology. "How did you find it?" Helgerson asked.

"I think a more appropriate question would be how did it get lost?"

"You never stop sniping, do you, Buccieri?"

"I'm already fired. What have I got to lose?"

"Just for the record," Helgerson said, raising his voice a bit, "I am *not* firing you because you are from the ghetto, because you are Italian, or because you are a woman."

Angela tucked the X rays tighter under her

arm and nodded her head in sarcastic agreement. "Oh, yeah? Then what goes on my record? I got fired because I bite my nails?"

"Try hostility to authority," Helgerson suggested as they turned the corner into radiology.

It took a few minutes to clip all of Mary Jane's X rays to the backlit panels. Then the machine whirred once, the panels rotated, and the baby bones appeared on the wall. A femur here, a tibia there—it was like a giant jigsaw puzzle.

"There they are," Dr. Greenberg announced. Three sets of trained eyes scanned the negatives. There was a long pause. They saw the recent fracture instantly. But here . . . on the left humerus. And the left tibia. And. . . .

"My God," said Helgerson softly.

Angela turned to an equally dumbstruck Dr. Greenberg. "Do I see three healed-over fractures, Doctor?"

"Yes, three."

Angela's lower jaw was set hard with anger. She could barely move it to say, "Sweet little Rowena Harper has broken her baby's body three times before this."

Dave Williams went about his job. He had talked to the maid and the mother and to half a dozen neighbors and friends of the Harpers with no break in the ice. As usual, no one was willing to risk a friendship, or an imagined lawsuit, by testifying that Rowena Harper abused her little girl. The fact that the court protected all such witnesses was a moot point with them —they didn't want the involvement. It was damned frustrating.

Once, when he was a teenager, he and some of his buddies had taken a camping trip up north along the beach near the mouth of the Rogue River. One day they decided to swim across, just for the hell of it. Dave was a good swimmer, but the current was very strong, and they'd forgotten to check the tide tables. When he was halfway across, some mental trigonometry told him he wasn't going to make it, that the current and tide would pull him out to sea before his feet would find the far bank. He altered course upstream and swam and swam as hard as he could.

He had made it, of course, but one sensation was firmly locked in his memory. As he neared the final ten feet of the seaward jetty, he began to probe with his feet for solid land. There was nothing to stand on. It *had* to be there, but it never rose to meet him. He finally had to pull himself, exhausted, hand over hand up the slippery rocks.

At times like this Dave remembered that experience. He knew the basic human dignity and decency were there, beneath the surface, but his feet could never find it. While he struggled, slowly, as if against tide and current, he was losing ground.

Brad and Nancy West lived right next door to the Harpers, and they had called the fire department the night of Mary Jane's abandonment. He'd tried three times before but never found them home. Mrs. West answered the door this time, and the expression on her face when he introduced himself told him he wasn't going to find bottom here either.

"Mrs. West, I am conducting a formal investigation for the Children's Protective Services in regards to allegations of child abuse and neglect against your neighbor, Mrs. Rowena Harper."

There was a trace of concern in Nancy West's face, but she was doing her best to conceal it. "We have nothing to say."

"You should know I am empowered to subpoena you into court if necessary."

Mrs. West quickly glanced over her shoulder into the house. Behind her Dave could see Mr. West, the man he'd talked to several weeks ago. Dave could see only the man's back, hunched over a small folding table as he ate lunch.

"Look," Nancy West continued, "my husband is retired because of his heart. He can't have any upset. Now we called the fire station when we saw smoke. We don't know anything at all about what else happened at that house. We never saw anything. We never heard anything. If you call us into court, you'll be wasting your time, as well as ours, and you'll be endangering my husband. Please—leave us alone."

"Nancy," said a weak voice inside, "close the door. I'm in a draft."

"I'm sorry," said Dave as the front door began to close on him.

A formal hearing into the matter of custody of Mary Jane Harper, a minor, convened in Room 205, juvenile court, of the Santa Carla County Courthouse on September 20. On her way to the hearing Angie Buccieri swung by the Children's Protective Services offices and picked up Dave Williams. They had been in touch several times during the course of Dave's investigation and had shared both the good and the bad news.

Neither had any idea what the outcome of the day's proceedings would be. If anything, Angie was a bit more optimistic than Dave; at least she had turned up some damaging evidence. As they drove, Dave nodded at the manila folder of X rays which Angie had tucked under her arm in a kind of instinctual protectiveness.

"Hold onto those X rays good and tight, doctor friend, because that there is our only evidence of actual abuse."

Angie's disgust was clear in her voice, too. "Swell."

"Neighbors heard nothing. Maid heard nothing. Grandmother knows nothing. . . ."

"And I was never a member of the Nazi Party," Angie concluded.

"Did you try to talk to Mary Jane?"

Angie closed her eyes briefly and nodded. "Forget it. God knows what she's feeling . . . but she is covering up for her mother in the only way she knows how. She won't talk."

"That is not unusual, Doctor. None of this is."

Angela pulled her cars into a parking space near the entrance to the courthouse, stuck the X rays resolutely under her arm, and marched up the long flight of wide steps to the courthouse entrance, her staccato gait keeping pace with Dave's two-at-a-time lope. "What about the husband?" she asked.

"Split to Mexico," Dave informed her. "No one knows where, of course."

"Of course."

Dave led her up the stairwell to the corridor he knew so well. As they rounded the last corner, however, Angie hesitated momentarily. There, just outside the courtroom's double doors, stood a thin, pale Rowena Harper. Before Dave could stop her, Angie was making a beeline for her. The courts might have their ways, and the state might have to observe certain legal procedures, but she was not bound by any of that. She had the evidence, and she knew she was right, and once, just once in her life, Rowena Harper was going to have to confront some ugly truth, face to face.

"Mrs. Harper?" Angela challenged.

Rowena looked up and saw the doctor. She recognized her at once. "Yes?" Her voice wavered.

When the time came, however, Angie could not formulate any stunning indictment. Whatever acid phrases she was counting on her anger to produce were choked by that very anger. Her sharp tongue found itself hung up on the lump in her throat, so that she could utter no more than one word.

"Why?" She flourished the bundle of X rays in Rowena's direction.

"All right, that's enough," said Mr. Bernard, who was standing next to his client.

"*Why?*" Angie demanded.

Her words sliced through Rowena with a force Angie had never expected. Her lips trembled visibly, and her bloodshot eyes began to mist. There was a deep reserve of guilt there, and Angie had just tapped the main pool. Despite herself, Dr. Buccieri felt a sudden sympathy for the confused young mother. As usual, Dave Williams had been right: They were not "monsters."

Mr. Bernard was fuming. "You say one more word to my client, and you are in serious trouble, young lady."

But Angie hardly heard him. She was consumed by her own moment of realization. "You're not the enemy either, are you?" she asked Rowena.

Mr. Bernard took charge of his client and steered her into the courtroom.

Dave waited patiently as Angela watched them disappear inside. "Well, who the hell is?" Angie finally asked an empty corridor. "Who the hell is?"

She was not to receive an answer inside. The facts were presented and Judge Carlson's eyes widened as the interpretation of the X rays was presented to him. Then Rowena's lawyer introduced Dr. Ernest Sutterman, a well-known local psychiatrist who testified on the progress Rowena was making with her problem.

Judge Carlson divided his gaze among the courtroom principals. "There is no doubt in the court's mind but that the allegations of abuse and neglect have been substantiated."

125

Angie and Dave looked at each other. They had done it even without the testimony of witnesses. But Dave was reserving any demonstration of satisfaction.

"However," the judge continued, "the court must take into consideration the supportive presence of Mrs. Harper's parents and the testimony of her psychiatrist, Dr. Sutterman, who finds her disturbed mental state temporary and responding to treatment. . . ."

Dave heard it coming: continuance.

Dr. Sutterman was a silver-haired man in the front row. He nodded in the judge's direction as if to reconfirm his prognosis.

"Court orders supervision of the Department of Social Services to continue and a more complete psychiatric evaluation by Dr. Sutterman within two months time."

"What's this?" Angela whispered.

"A continuance. He's not going to decide today."

"What?"

Okay, Dave said to himself. Your Honor's playing it safe. Your Honor needs more data. But what about the child?

"At that hearing the question of legal custody of the minor child, Mary Jane Harper, will be decided."

*Who* gets custody?

126

"Until then physical custody of the minor child is returned to her mother."

"All rise! The Juvenile Court of the County of Santa Carla is now adjourned."

# CHAPTER

# X

Dr. Helgerson looked up from his paperwork when he heard a knock at his door. "Come in."

Angela Buccieri entered. She stood in front of his desk for a moment, twisting her stethoscope in her hands. Her eyes were full of tears.

"Your side won, Dr. Helgerson," she said. Despite the tears, her tone was matter-of-fact, like that of a world-weary journalist reporting more casualties. Ever more casualties. . . .

"Your friend's little girl has her baby back. The lawyer her family bought fixed it. The psychiatrist her family bought says she has this little temporary nervous problem during which she broke four of her baby's bones and burned her a couple times, but all that unpleasant stuff is over now." Angela was trying to be sarcastic, trying to mimic what she figured they must be saying over tea at the women's Wednesday luncheon at the country club. But sarcasm wasn't working; her voice was cracking. "Mommy is going to be just fine now. Of course, Mary Jane has, in her thirty-six months of life on this earth, been beaten, tortured, and left to burn up. *She* may not be fine. She doesn't talk anymore, and she may never talk again as a result of all this trauma so in fact, we may never know the whole story of what has been done to her.

"But what the hell, she's not our property, is she? She the *property* of her mother. That's who she *belongs* to, just like any other small, dumb animal, right? And like an animal, Mary Jane Harper has no real value. She can't vote."

Dr. Helgerson was not one to accept the blame for society's ills. He didn't feel guilty for slavery or discrimination or the plight of migrant farm workers just because he happened to be white, professional, and prosperous. You couldn't lay that on him. He'd tell you it was a cheap radical trick to try. But he didn't say anything now, and Angela thought she saw traces of guilt on his face, as much as that solid Scandinavian face would show.

"Have you got it all out?" Helgerson asked, trying to be firm.

"Not quite. I've decided not to let you fire me, Dr. Helgerson. You try and I'll fight you in the courts. It's not that I'm crazy about this place, but you need someone like me here, and I do a great job." She paused, clearing her throat. "For the sake of our working relationship, I'll try to improve my professional attitude."

Helgerson leaned back in his chair and lit his pipe. "That's very good of you, Doctor."

"The county offers training for doctors in suspected child abuse and neglect detection. Several of us are going to take it. We intend to be much more cautious around here, Dr. Helgerson."

Helgerson removed the pipe stem from his mouth. He looked Angela squarely in the eye. "You can get off your high horse now, Doctor. I'm taking that training, too."

Angela returned his gaze. Then she smiled and quietly left the office.

She was feeling better now. Her chosen profession hadn't let her down after all. And if she were still looking for an enemy on the issue of child abuse, she would have to keep looking— the man in the big office wasn't the one.

Rowena's nervous laughter filled the office. Her right hand flipped back and forth in a "who cares" gesture. She was desperately lighthearted.

"Okay. So daddy was crazy about me, and Mommy was jealous. Big deal. What else is new?"

A massive slab of waxed mahogany separated Rowena from Dr. Sutterman. The psychiatrist leaned back in his large leather chair and stared abstractedly at his patient. The chair was designed with large circular wings on either side of Dr. Sutterman's head, making him look like a medieval pontiff. His desk was custom-built, with recesses for built-in tape recorders and a polygraph, each covered with a stylish smoked-glass panel. The doctor said nothing.

"I've been running my rotten story for six weeks, Dr. Sutterman. I hope you're getting a good book from all this. You always want to know what I feel. You never tell me what you're thinking."

"What would you like to hear, Rowena?"

"Your *feelings*. Like the people at Parents Anonymous. I mean, at least they *talked* to me. Why can't I go back there?"

The doctor leaned forward in his leather cocoon. "We've discussed this before, Rowena. You're here by court order. Now. Shall we go on? . . . Your mother confronted you sitting on your father's lap in your underwear when you were seven. She suspected sexual foreplay. She grew angry. And then?"

*And then. . . .* The shadows danced, became clear, shimmered in their illumination.

"Well, the whole thing was really very gross," Rowena began, nervously flippant. "Daddy's way of handling a scene was to go off on the boat, so he took a long weekend, whereupon darling Mama . . . darling Mama. . . ."

*Mommy, don't look at me like that! Please, Mommy. . . .*

"Mama locked me in the closet to punish me."

*Please, Mommy.*

"She pushed me up the stairs and locked me in that closet."

Rowena reached for a cigarette, beginning to tremble.

*You're a bad girl. Bad.*

*No, Mommy. It's cold. Please. So dark and cold.*

*And stay in there until you can be good.*

"It was so dark and cold in there. I reached up. I was so small I had to stretch . . . reached up to some boxes. I was looking for some winter clothes to keep warm. I reached up and—"

*Eyes!*

"It was a rat. A big rat! It ran right down my arm!"

132

*Mommy!*

"I could see him in the corner looking at me. His eyes . . . big and black. I was so scared I wet my pants. . . ."

*Mommy, please! It's here. It's in here. Eyes!*

"I yelled for my mommy to let me out. I kept screaming, 'Oh, please, let me out of here, please, Mommy. I'll tell the truth.' Daddy just wanted—"

*Ahoy, little girl. . . .*

"Daddy just wanted me to touch him, that's all! Just touch him. That's the truth."

*Eyes! Big and black, like Mommy's, accusing me, staring at me. . . .*

Rowena was sobbing, writhing in the sudden onslaught of guilt and memory. Dr. Sutterman was writing on his pad when a small buzzer sounded inside his wristwatch.

"Our time is up, Rowena. We'll go on with this on Wednesday."

Rowena couldn't stop crying. "That's the truth. I tried to tell her, but she—"

"We'll get into it next time, Rowena. Our time is now *up*."

"He said it wasn't anything bad. I didn't know. Why wouldn't she let me out of the closet? I . . . *It* was in there."

Dr. Sutterman rose from his desk and crossed to the office door. "You think about that, and we'll talk about it on Wednesday."

He opened the door, showing her the way out. The open door had an effect on Rowena; the real world came back into focus again. She sensed the secretary in the antechamber and other patients waiting. She blinked, then turned her head to find the source of the doctor's voice. "Please, Dr. Sutterman, can't I talk to you a little more right now?"

"No more time today, Rowena. See you Wednesday."

"Yes. Sure. . . ."

Rowena found her way home on remote control. The brush with her deepest fears and memories had greatly unbalanced her. There had to be something she could do, some way to escape. She couldn't go back to Sutterman. She couldn't relive that again.

*Eyes.* . . .

No, not again. She would have to . . . have to do something. *Go* somewhere. That was it! Leave all this . . . this pressure and find a new place. Sure, that was it. With Mary Jane, someplace away from all the courts and doctors and social workers and mothers—*that* was the place for the two of them.

Safe. Safe from the eyes.

The baby-sitter was reading a magazine in the living room when Rowena arrived home. Mary Jane was in her miniature chair in front of the television.

"Hi. Everything go okay?"

"Just fine," said the teenage girl. "Mary Jane never made a sound."

Rowena smiled. Then she dug into her purse and shakily snatched some money out for the girl.

"Are you okay, Mrs. Harper?"

Rowena froze a smile onto her face. "Sure, fine. Thanks, hon. See you Wednesday."

When the sitter was gone, Rowena collapsed onto the sofa with a large drink. The house still smelled like smoke, even after all this time. These things just keep following you, like smoke, following you and following you until you blow them away. Until you get away from them, like out in the desert, where it was clean and there was always a big wind. Someplace remote. Bill liked the desert. That was it. Just drive and drive and find Bill.

*Let me out, Mommy, please. . . .*

Mary Jane looked in Rowena's direction. Rowena felt her eyes on her and looked up.

"We're going bye-bye, Mary Jane." She poured herself another drink and paced the room, lighting a fresh cigarette. "See, we can't stay here anymore. It's too dangerous. I tell you what—maybe we'll go find Daddy. Would you like that? Mary Jane? Should we try to go find our daddy?"

*Don't look at me like that. . . .*

*Don't. . . .*

Mary Jane saw her mother's face change. The sweetness disappeared; the coldness returned. The child couldn't help reacting. Her large eyes grew wider with the anticipation of punishment. Her mother was screaming at her.

"Stop that! Stop looking at me like that! Stop it!"

Rowena came toward her child, and Mary Jane started crying. But she was lucky this time—Rowena had escape, not punishment, on her mind. Mary Jane was yanked from the tiny chair and stuffed into a small red coat.

"Come on. Quick. We'll go find our daddy."

They were out the door and driving away within five minutes.

Half an hour later the phone at the Harper house began to ring. It rang fifteen times with no answer.

In his office Dave Williams hung up. The court had ordered supervision of the Harper home. When he couldn't get an answer there, he began to worry. He instantly punched another number from the case file. The party he got at the other end was not pleased to hear his voice.

"No, Mr. Williams," Thomas J. Atherton said with a certain exasperation, "Rowena is not here. What is this now? Are we going to be harrassed every time Rowena goes out to the market or maybe takes Mary Jane to Pioneer Park?"

"I am sorry to disturb you, Mr. Atherton. But the court ordered continuing supervision, and I take that to mean knowing where your daughter and her little girl have gone. If I don't, you should."

"Listen to me," Atherton growled, "and listen good: My grandchild is well, and so is my daughter. In just two days this whole matter will be closed. Dr. Sutterman tells me Rowena has been making excellent progress, and he is going to recommend that all supervision be terminated. One less case for you and your bleeding-heart cohorts to use as an excuse to sponge off the taxpayers' money."

Atherton slammed the phone in Dave's ear. Dave held the receiver away from his head and curled a silent four-letter word in its direction. Okay, he thought, I've got only two days. In those two days, I'm gonna be the nosiest sponge you ever saw.

He drove to Rowena's house. The driveway was empty, and the doorbell chimed without result. Dave even went so far as to peer in the living-room windows, but no one was home. When he finally lifted the garage door, his suspicions were confirmed: Rowena had taken flight with Mary Jane.

Dave had a big decision to make. He was within his rights to call the police at this point. Certainly no one could fault his reasoning. But perhaps Atherton, despite his bomb-them-into-the-Stone-Age politics, was reporting things accurately. If Rowena *was* making progress with her psychiatrist, this disappearance might be a trial balloon, a weekend or even a single night away from the house with her child. Of course, Rowena was required to clear any such trips, but maybe she had forgotten or was ignorant of the procedure. Or perhaps she had left the required itinerary with her psychiatrist. The psychiatrist might even have suggested the trip.

Back at his office Dave dialed Dr. Sutterman's number. It rang five times before his answering service picked it up. "Is this his service?" Dave asked. "I see. This is Dave Williams, Children's Protective Services. The number is 555-7692. Would you ask Dr. Sutterman to call me as soon as you hear from him? I'll give you my home number, too."

By the time Dave was ready to leave for the day it was almost seven. Dr. Sutterman had not returned his call, and he was still of two minds. The Santa Carla police were very good and discreet in cases like this. So was the highway patrol. On the other hand, Dave could picture the first, pleasant, nonthreatening weekend Rowena and her child had shared in years

138

being shattered by the arrival of a uniform with orders from the court. It might set Rowena's progress as a parent back months.

He decided to let it ride until morning. His gut resisted the idea mightily, but in the end his hope won out.

Mary Jane was petrified in the passenger's seat. Her mommy was driving the car crazy.

"Mommy. . . ."

"Be quiet. We're going to find Daddy, so be quiet."

Rowena felt eyes studying her. She snapped her gaze off the road and caught Mary Jane in her favorite trick.

"Don't! Don't look at me! Look at the scenery."

"Mommy!"

Rowena's red car had drifted into the oncoming lane of traffic. A camper was headed directly for them, horn blaring. . . .

Rowena swerved just in time and slammed into the side of the camper. Mary Jane began to cry.

"Be quiet! It's all right. . . ."

The camper skidded into the center dividing lane. The driver bounced out, but the red car was speeding away from him, clearly not intending to stop. He reached into the cab and got some paper and a pencil and recorded Rowena's license plate number.

Lady, the man thought, I hope you get where you're going.

# XI

There was a framed print of an ugly seascape on the peeling walls. In one corner a scarred and burned writing table listed against a broomstick which had been taped to the stump of a long-broken leg. There was a double bed which took up most of the floor space in the tiny room. The motel room exuded the scent of hasty lovemaking, furtive encounters. Part of the bathtub in the tiny bathroom was abrased down to the metal—the backs of soldiers from nearby Fort Thompson, the backs of whores from the nearby honky-tonk town of El Conte.

Rowena saw none of it. The shadows were closing over everything. Gray. It was all gray.

Rowena paced back and forth in the tiny

room, filling the undersized glass ashtrays with butts. It wasn't working. There was no escape here. The reason was sitting on the plastic bed- spread, whimpering, curled into a pathetic little ball.

"Daddy . . . Daddy," Mary Jane whim- pered softly.

*Ahoy, little girl.*

"Daddy. . . ."

Rowena's face was tight. She marched over to her child sitting on the bed. "Daddy's not here," she screamed. And then, softer, like one child taunting another: "You see, Daddy's not anywhere. I guess he went sailing the ocean blue. And he'd rather be with me than with you."

Mary Jane stopped her whimpering. Her black eyes grew wide with fear.

"No," Rowena whimpered and backed away. "Stop looking at me like that!"

Past and present images connected in Rowena's mind. Mary Jane's eyes grew larger, larger; her form grew until it filled the bed. . . .

*It's in here! Mommy! Eyes!*

Her little face sprouted whiskers; her little hands became . . . became. . . .

The glistening eyes of a rat stared back at her.

"No! Go away and leave me alone," Rowena screamed. She backed away from the bed,

142

clawing at the wall. No escape—she'd brought it with her. *It* was here.

*Let me out!*

"Leave me alone!"


Judy was one flight down from her apartment. She was on her way home with some groceries for that night's Parents Anonymous meeting when she heard her phone ringing. She dashed up the stairs, fumbled with the keys and the paper bag until she managed to get in and lift the receiver.

"Hello?"

There was a child crying piteously in the background.

"Hello? Who is this?"

"This is Rowena," cried a voice on the other end.

"Yes, Rowena. You were here a couple of months ago. We were hoping to hear from you again."

In the motel room Mary Jane's crying was penetrating Rowena like a thousand needles. . . .

Rowena's voice was wavering with anger and confusion. "She won't stop crying. I can't make her shut up. You . . . you make her shut up. Okay?"

Judy could hear a crisis situation, could feel Rowena's hysteria. She swiftly retrieved a pen and pad from her desk. Her moves, her decisions were critical at this moment.

"Now listen, Rowena. You are not alone. Do you hear? We care about you. Tell me where you are, and I'll come right over. Where do you live?"

Rowena was too confused to think. Where was she? In this room here. With this noise, this . . . these eyes looking at her. "I'm not at home. I don't know where I am. In the desert somewhere. . . . Some motel. . . ."

"Do you know how long you were driving?" Judy asked.

"I don't know. Maybe an hour. . . ." Then Judy heard a change in her voice. It sent a chill through her. "She won't stop crying, you see. I need for it to be quiet now, so I can think."

What was that change? Rowena seemed calmer as she said it, almost as if her mind were seeking a logical reason for making the child be quiet. Abusing a child out of confusion or hysteria was one thing. But when the parent began seeking and finding logical reasons, a much more dangerous condition was setting in.

The condition had a name: psychosis.

There was a knock at Judy's apartment door, and she was very relieved to see Joy and Billie Rae poke their heads around the open door.

She frantically gestured "come in" to them. "Rowena, is there a name of the motel anywhere in the room? Look on your key, Rowena."

Key? The key to the door. Yes, where was it? God, the crying was getting louder. I can't think like this. I can't. . . . "I don't know. Please make her stop crying!"

Judy clapped her hand over the phone and handed Billie Rae a card with Dave Williams' number on it. "Bang on doors in this place till you find a phone. Get Dave Williams. . . . Rowena something-or-other is in big trouble. She's freaking out with her kid in a motel somewhere in the desert about an hour from here. Call the police, too. I'll try to hold her."

Billie Rae and Joy scurried out into the hallway.

"Rowena," Judy continued. "Listen to me, hon. . . . Now, I'm gonna stay with you."

"Okay, okay," replied a small voice.

"Okay. Let's take three deep breaths together. Good deep ones. . . . One . . . two . . . three. . . ."

Judy could hear Rowena exhale into the phone. The stream of air was vibrating against the mouthpiece. She could imagine the violent tremors of the young mother's rib cage.

"Good. Now that's better. Okay, now leave

145

the phone off the hook and I'll stay here. You go to the motel manager. You remember him? You signed the register. Tell him you're sick and need help. Tell him to call me, and I'll come and get you."

"Yes. Please come get me."

The child's crying built to a new level. It seemed loud and nerve-racking even through the long-distance connection.

"Get me out of here! Make her stop!"

It wasn't working. Rowena was losing control. She wasn't listening.

"Rowena! Do what I tell you. Go to the motel manager right now. Tell him you need help. Tell him to call the police. . . ."

Idiot! Why did you say that word?

"Rowena?"

There was a short pause. "No, no. No police. They don't like bad girls. They lock them up in closets. . . . No."

The line went dead.

Dave Williams was at home when Billie Rae called. "Hello? Yeah! . . . Oh, God. . . . The desert? *Where* in the desert? . . . Okay, I'm on it. Thanks."

He fired up his car and drove swiftly to the local police station. Billie Rae had called the station before he got there. The desk sergeant had a patrol car waiting with an officer. He also had a possible lead.

Mary Jane was howling. She wanted out of that dirty place, back in her crib. She wanted her daddy.

The room blistered with the noise. Rowena couldn't think. She couldn't light a cigarette. There was no liquor, no friends, no escape. . . .

Rowena sprang over to the lumpy bed. "You have to stop doing that. You have to stop crying!"

She sat down on the bed next to her child. "You have to obey me. Do what I say. Stop making trouble all the time."

Rowena clapped her hand firmly over Mary Jane's mouth. The child was struggling, but listen—no crying. The voices stopped. She could think. That was it. Make the crying go away, and she could . . . could. . . .

"I want you to go away and leave me alone now," Rowena said to Mary Jane. The silence was wonderful. She leaned back to enjoy it. But Mary Jane was still struggling. Rowena's hand rested on the bed pillow. Her fist grabbed a bunch of it. She lifted it toward Mary Jane's struggling form.

"I want it to be quiet now, okay? Just be quiet and sleep."

She put the pillow over Mary Jane's face. Firmly. To make it quiet.

"We really got lucky," the police officer told Dave as they climbed into the patrol car. "The guy she hit on the highway got her number. Called it into the highway patrol. I think I know the area. Out near Fort Thompson. There's a string of motels out there."

"A string of motels?" Dave asked, discouraged.

The patrol car squealed its tires out of the station as the officer hit the siren and lights. "We'll find the right one."

With lights and siren, speeds approaching eighty, and an escort part of the way from the California highway patrol, it took Dave and the officer about forty minutes to reach the town of El Conte. Dave was further discouraged, however, when he saw what seemed like an endless string of cheap wooden motels lining the highway.

They had passed about five of them when Dave's eye caught a glimpse of red metal parked behind one of the motel offices.

"Hold it. Back up a little."

The officer reversed gears and backed up about ten yards. Dave got the portable spotlight from the dashboard rack and played it across the front of a motel. When it finally reached around a corner, there was a red convertible with license plate numbers which matched Rowena's.

"That's it."

Rowena had turned off all the motel room lights but one. Over that one she had draped a lavender scarf. The diffused purple light soothed the quiet room. She cradled her baby girl in her arms on the edge of the bed, gently rocking her, softly singing. She had undressed her child for nap time, and the child's pale, little arms fell limply at her side.

> Hush, little baby,
> Don't say a word,
> Mommy's gonna buy you
> A mockingbird. . . .

The motel door crunched open under the foot of the police officer. Dave Williams dashed inside and then stopped in his tracks. Slowly he circled the bed to where Rowena sat.

> If that mockingbird
> Don't sing,
> Mommy's gonna buy you
> A diamond ring. . . .

Rowena never looked up. Her eyes were

149

locked on the stiff, unmoving bundle in her arms, which she rocked back and forth, ever so gently.

Dave felt his stomach muscles contract.

# CHAPTER

# XII

Judge Carlson arrived in his chambers late the next morning. "I don't know," he complained to his secretary. "Seems to me the traffic gets worse every month."

He carefully hung his suit coat on a hanger and donned his robe. The secretary placed a cup of coffee on his desk, and the judge settled down to a pile of file folders. "What's first this morning?"

"The Harper case," said his secretary.

"Right. Did the psychiatric evaluation come in?"

"Uh, yes. Late yesterday." She fished it out of the mail packet. "Here you go."

Carlson looked over the three-page report.

The court often consulted Dr. Sutterman, a fact which made this decision easier—Sutterman knew what the judge needed to know. Yes, it was all here.

The desk phone rang, and the secretary picked it up. "Judge Carlson's chambers."

"This looks good," the judge said. "I think we can terminate supervision here."

He looked up when the secretary made no response. Her face bore a disturbed expression as she replaced the phone.

"Judge?" she said.

"What is it?"

"Mary Jane Harper died last night."

Some children, they say, give you no clue. But this was not the case with Mary Jane Harper. It was all there, the whole blueprint . . . to the eye which cared enough to look.

# About the Author

Joanna Lee, author of MARY JANE HARPER CRIED LAST NIGHT and I WANT TO KEEP MY BABY!, was a teenage mother, but was divorced at age twenty. When her second marriage ended, Ms. Lee resumed her TV writing career. She had already been a model, actress, and comedy writer. After turning out numerous TV dramas, she became story executive on the show "Room 222." She later formed her own production company, Christiana Productions. She became the first American woman to write, direct, produce, and star in a feature-length motion picture, "A Pocket Filled with Dreams" (Cannes Film Festival, 1975).

Ms. Lee has received two Writers Guild of America nominations and won an Emmy Award for "The Waltons Thanksgiving Special." She wrote "Cage without a Key," and was writer as well as associate producer of "Babe," which received ten Emmy nominations. She has received a Golden Globe Award and a Christopher Award. In addition to writing I WANT TO KEEP MY BABY! and MARY JANE HARPER CRIED LAST NIGHT, she was the producer of both films.

# 045

# HEARTWARMING STORIES BY JOHN NEUFELD

☐ **TWINK by John Neufield.** An unforgettable, deeply felt novel of a cou ageous handicapped girl and the world of love she created. Docto told Twink's mother how hopeless her daughter's case was. But ho could any of them give up on Twink or stop loving her—when sh refused to give up either on them or herself? "Beautiful!"—*Des Moin Register* (159551—$2.9

☐ **EDGAR ALLAN.** In this penetrating novel, John Neufeld examines th problems that arise when a white middle class family adopts a bla child. (167759—$3.5

☐ **LISA, BRIGHT AND DARK.** Lisa is slowly going mad but her symptom even an attempted suicide, fail to alert her parents or teachers to h illness. She finds compassion only from three girlfriends who bar together to provide what they call "group therapy." (166841—$3.5

Prices slightly higher in Canada

_____

Buy them at your local bookstore or use this convenient coupon for ordering.

**NEW AMERICAN LIBRARY**
**P.O. Box 999, Bergenfield, New Jersey 07621**

Please send me the books I have checked above. I am enclosing $_____
(please add $1.00 to this order to cover postage and handling). Send chec or money order—no cash or C.O.D.'s. Prices and numbers are subject to chang without notice.

Name_____

Address_____

City _____ State _____ Zip Code _____
Allow 4-6 weeks for delivery.
This offer is subject to withdrawal without notice.